What reviewers are saying about the stories in Catari Heat

Catari Heat 1: New Beginnings

"Catari Heat 1: New Beginnings by Kyla Logan is the beginning of a paranormal series that is very unique. Ms. Logan's ideas are fun and written with a "freshness". I enjoyed Leah in that she wasn't going to simply do what was expected without some explanation. And Darius is such an Alpha hero, yet with a tenderness toward Leah that is wonderful to see! Their Mating Ceremony was absolutely wonderfully romantic! I would recommend this book to anyone!"

-- PamL, A Romance Review

Catari Heat 2: Double the Pleasure

"Double The Pleasure is an exciting tale of two very sensual brothers that will rock readers' worlds and steam their windows. Jarod and Jeran are erotic and passionate creatures who will curl your toes and leave you panting. Ashley is strong willed, but can't help but be drawn by the desire she feels for Jeran and Jarod. Kyla Logan has penned another winner in this shape-shifting tale of adventure and love. I can't wait to see what the next book in the series reveals about the sensual shape-shifters."

-- Angel Brewer, The Romance Studio

Catari Heat 3: Mate Fever

"This book is full of passion, action and adventure that will keep the readers turning the pages until the very end. The love scenes are intense and have a fiery heat that will singe your hair. Kyla Logan has penned the perfect ending to this wonderful series and I can't wait to see what her creative mind comes up with next."

-- Angel, The Romance Studio

www.ChangelingPress.com

Catari Heat

Kyla Logan

ISBN: 978-1-59596-484-7

Publisher:
Changeling Press LLC
PO Box 1046
Martinsburg, WV 25402-1046
www.ChangelingPress.com

Printed in the U.S.A.
Lightning Source, Inc.
1246 Heil Quaker Blvd
La Vergne TN 37086
www.lightningsource.com

Anthology Editor: Maryam Salim
Cover Artist: Angela Knight
Cover Layout: Bryan Keller

The individual stories in this anthology have been previously released in E-Book format.

Catari Heat 1: New Beginnings

Kyla Logan

Chapter One

"I can't believe this is going to be our last mission ever, Ash. It's not fair that we have to stop flying once we're mated, but males can keep on piloting," Leah said for about the thousandth time.

"I hate it as much as you, but we have to accept it. Don't give me that look." Ashley turned away to look at her control panel.

"I know. Sorry. I don't know what is wrong with me. I haven't been sleeping well. I wish I had more time to get to know Jason before we're mated." Leah sighed and turned back to her instrument panel, buckling herself into her harness. "Prepare to come out of leeway."

Leah slowed the shuttle down as they approached the planet. "Orbit is stabilised," announced the voice of the onboard computer.

Ashley unclipped her harness and moved around her control panel, ready to start collecting readings. "I don't believe this."

Leah turned around, worried by the shaky tone in Ashley's voice. She was staring at the planet in front of them with a stunned expression on her face. Raising one hand she pointed at the screen. "That is the planet I have been dreaming of, I am sure of it."

"How is that possible? I thought you were just having erotic dreams." Leah turned back to look at the planet, wondering why Ash had dreamed of a place she'd never seen before.

The computer blared out a warning. "Instrument failure, orbit destabilising."

"Get yourself buckled up again," Leah shouted as they fought to stabilise the shuttle, but the situation was hopeless. One way or another they were landing on the surface of this planet.

* * *

Leah groaned as she came to. Her head pounded, her sides ached. The pain made it hard to concentrate, to remember what had happened, to figure out where she was.

Curls of smoke rose and bright sparks shot from the damaged wires and circuit boards. The burning smell stung her nose as she unclipped the safety harness holding her in the pilot's chair and carefully stood up, holding her sore ribs as she did. When the shuttle crashed, she'd been flung forward in the safety harness. Although it had saved her from serious injury it had bruised her sides.

"Ashley!" Leah shouted.

What a mess! Anything that hadn't been secured was scattered all over the floor. Stepping over the ruined equipment as quickly as she could, she headed to the back of the shuttle looking for Ashley.

Leah found her friend beside the damaged control panel console, one arm at an unnatural angle half in the safety harness. Kneeling by her side Leah pressed her fingers to the warm skin of her throat. There was a pulse. Weak, but still a pulse. *Thank Skyla*! Leah gently moved Ashley so she lay flat on the floor of the shuttle. Straightening Ashley's arm as much as she could, she made her as comfortable as possible for the moment, but her friend needed help and fast.

Taking a deep breath, she willed herself to focus. Picking her way through the wreckage, she made her way to the storage compartments for the mediKit. Rounding the corner she stopped abruptly. The medi compartment door hung wide open. Bits of the mediKit lay scattered in broken pieces on the floor.

Slumping against the bulkhead, Leah closed her eyes, wondering what on Skyla she could do for Ashley now. Feeling light-headed from the pain in her ribs, she searched for something she could use to immobilise Ashley's arm, but found nothing. The mediKit would have fixed her broken bones in a second. She'd have to create a makeshift splint instead. Ripping up some of their uniforms would provide the only strapping she would be able to use as binding on a splint for the broken arm.

Moving back through the litter and debris, Leah went into the sleeping quarters. Clothing was thrown everywhere. Only after she had ripped the shirts into strips did she realise that there was nothing on board the shuttle that she could use as a splint. She remembered seeing wooded areas as the shuttle had crash-landed. Maybe she could find some sticks or branches to use outside the ship. At least she knew the atmosphere was breathable from the few readings they had been able to gather before the systems failure.

Leah made her way back to Ashley's side. *Thank Skyla*! Her pulse was a bit stronger, but Ashley's arm was swelling quickly. She needed to strap it as soon as possible. Going to the exit, Leah entered the combination for the door. Nothing. She tried again. Damn. It barely opened far enough for her to slip out. Wincing at the pain in her side, Leah squeezed her body through the narrow opening. Misjudging how much force she needed to use to push the door open further, she fell forwards. Screaming, her heart lurching, she tumbled through the air.

Leah gasped as she slammed into the hard body of a man. Tears came to her eyes when his strong, muscular arms came around her, causing agony. Leah opened her eyes and lifted her head off the bare chest of the man who had broken her fall. She stared down into the deepest blue eyes she'd ever seen. A woman could drown in eyes like those.

And he wasn't alone. Out of the corner of her eye she spotted lots of feet, feet attached to long, long legs. Attempting to push herself up from the man she was sprawled across, she felt the heat and hardness of his erection.

Well, he's happy to see me, she thought, annoyed and a little frightened when he wouldn't release her. Who was he?

But more importantly why was her body responding to his? Ripples of pleasure coursed through her body, her nipples drawing into tight buds as they pressed against her uniform. Her pussy ground against the growing hardness of his cock as she stimulated it unintentionally, trying to make him release her. She took a closer look at him, trying not to let him know she was studying him intently, wanting to figure out what was causing her body to react to him in this disconcerting way.

His glossy, jet-black hair looked like silk, and it cried out for her to run her fingers through it. *Where on Skyla did that thought come from*? He had a firm, hard jaw and his lips were fuller than she was used to seeing on the males of her people. Strange, but on him they looked just right. His scent was musky male combined with… was that vanilla? What an unusual combination.

She had a strong feeling she could trust him, although why she felt this instinctively she didn't know. The men surrounding them all had dark hair, in varying lengths. They wore garments similar to loincloths, very brief, that left little to her imagination. Not that she needed an imagination since she was lying on one of them feeling every broad inch of him.

She pushed as firmly as she could against his shoulder again, but she could not get away from him. He was like a brick wall of muscle, only oh, so warm under her fingers. Sparks ran through her hands where she touched him.

Her pussy grew warm and wet, as if her body was preparing itself for him. Her nipples, already hard points, seemed to tighten even more as they pressed against the hard planes of his chest. She must have suffered from a concussion. That was the only logical explanation for the strange reaction of her body. She couldn't physically move him, so she decided to try to influence him by telepathy. Such actions were frowned on by her people but she was desperate to distance herself from him.

All she met was a blank spot. Leah moaned at the violent pain that shot through her head as she tried to link with his mind. *What on Skyla is going on? How is he able to block me?* She should have been able to make him release her without his knowledge, without his being aware of her presence in his mind. But the frown on his face showed he was aware of her attempt.

* * *

Darius winced at the sharp sensation of a touch aimed at his mind. It felt like an attack so he quickly put up barriers against intrusion.

He looked up into his mate's eyes, seeing pain and something else he didn't recognise shining back at him. Whatever it was, he didn't like it. It had looked like disgust for a moment in time, something he had not expected his mate to feel at being held by him.

And there was no doubt in his mind that this was *her*, a mate who was not looking all that pleased to see him… or his people.

When the Seer told him she would arrive soon, he'd wondered if that would be good for his people. He was their leader and to have a life mate who was an outsider, one who did not know their ways, could be difficult for them all. She would have to make a lot of changes in her life, and from the look in her eyes she would fight him all the way. That was something he could not allow to happen. Unity between alphas was what every pack needed.

"Please, you have to let me get up," said his mate. "My friend is injured and she needs help."

"Kell, take some of the men and check on the girl," he said. He stood, still holding her closely in his arms.

"You can put me down now," she said with a little tremor in her voice.

"Oh, I think that would be a bad idea. You look like you are going to collapse. Tell me what you are called and how we can understand each other's speech."

"My name is Leah. I am of the Skylian people. Ashley and I were taking readings of your planet when something went wrong and we crashed on your world. I have a translator chip inserted behind my ear that allows me to simultaneously understand and speak your language."

"I am honoured to meet you, Leah. I am Darius, of the Leopai people of Catari. Come. I will take you to my home so your injuries can be properly tended."

"I can't leave until I find out how Ashley is. Please." She tried desperately to wriggle free of his grip.

"Shh, it's okay. Let me take care of you. My men will bring your friend. It is you I am worried about." With that he strode toward a horse-like creature. Its body was white with black stripes marking its coat.

Darius sat astride the animal, holding Leah close to his chest, delighting in the close contact with his mate. Gently using his knees he guided the animal in the direction of his stronghold.

Chapter Two

Darius entered his room, crossed to the side of the sleeping pallet and looked down at his mate. How beautiful she was, her oval-shaped face with high cheekbones. Her golden blonde hair was cut short now. She would of course grow it longer to a style in keeping with the traditional Leopai female.

The top of her head only reached his chest when she stood, and that made him feel protective of her. However he had an idea from their earlier encounter that she would not accept his authority over her with good grace. He smiled; she would soon find out what it meant to be the mate of a Leopai male.

Sitting down at the edge of the pallet, he carefully moved the cover to her waist, so as not to awaken her. Knowing he was taking unfair advantage, he still had to see her, to touch her, to convince himself she was actually here with him. He had waited for her a long, long time.

He was glad Mata had removed Leah's torn uniform to heal her. Now he could see all of her. Gently tracing his finger around the areola of one of her breasts, he watched her nipple grow into a hard point. Unable to resist, he bent his head and licked the edge with the tip of his tongue. Leah moved restlessly on the pallet, but stilled when nothing else disturbed her sleep.

Darius could not believe such a brief taste made him harder. He had been hard since he entered the room. Now his cock felt like a steel post! But he had to taste her again… no matter the cost in discomfort to himself.

Chapter Three

Leah was in agony. She heard footsteps approach the sleeping pallet where Darius held her in his arms. She had never before felt so protected; it was a strange feeling for her. Although she knew she should not have such thoughts, there was something about him that called to something deep inside of her. Perhaps it was his scent or the way he made her feel when she was with him, safe and cherished.

A female appeared in front of them, holding a goblet in her hands.

"My Lady, I have a potion that will take your pain away. Please drink this." She held it up to Leah's mouth, carefully making sure she did not allow any to spill. The tangy drink tasted of citrus and was not unpleasant at all.

To Leah's surprise the pain in her head receded quickly. She faced the woman, noticing her beauty, with her long black hair and delicate features.

"I feel better, thank you." Leah inclined her head in a slight bow, then turned to Darius. "But, please, tell me what you meant by saying I was your mate?"

"We can talk about that when you feel better."

Leah noticed the woman looking intently at Darius. She did not like the feeling of possessiveness that came over her at the thought there was some link between them. She found herself gripping his arm with no knowledge of when she placed her hand there. She felt so confused with these unwanted feelings. She had to focus on something else. "Ashley! I must find out how my friend is. Can you take me to her?"

"Your friend is still unconscious, my Lady. I have tended to her injuries. We must wait for her to awaken on her own," said the woman in a low and gentle tone.

"Why are you calling me 'my lady'? Wait! It doesn't matter just now, just take me to Ashley. I have to see for myself that she is comfortable."

As Darius stood up she felt him give a big sigh. *What is the matter with him*? Leah blushed when she realised she'd been sitting on his knee, naked! It seemed that just his touch had destroyed her normal clear thinking.

Thankfully the woman produced a tunic and helped Leah slip it on. Just that activity exhausted Leah, and she was grateful when Darius picked her up in his strong, muscular arms once more. *She could get used to this*!

"I will take you to her room so you can see for yourself that she is sleeping and has been tended to. This is Mata, our Seer. She will answer any questions you have."

Leah was aware of long corridors and high ceilings as he carried her toward a different area of his home. Mata crossed in front of them and opened the door to another room.

As he strode through the opening, she saw Ashley lying on a sleeping pallet with a bandage around her head and a splint on her arm. A woman was sitting beside the pallet, watching over Ashley.

The woman rose to her feet when they entered the room, smiling at Leah. Or the smile might have been directed at Darius, she didn't know.

"She has not awakened yet, Mata, but she appears to be comfortable," said the woman.

"That will be all for the moment, Kara. Go and refresh yourself. Come back in thirty minutes. We shall be here till then," said the Seer as she walked over to the sleeping pallet.

"Her recordings are still stable. We just have to have patience until she wakens. Until then all we can do is make her comfortable." Mata turned back to face Darius and Leah.

Darius carried Leah to the chair beside the pallet and carefully sat her on it. Leah looked at her friend, feeling much better now that she could see for herself how Ashley was doing.

She didn't like the pale and drawn look to Ashley's face. Ashley's breathing was shallow, and she had a terrible bruise spreading down the right side of her face. Her shoulder-length hair had been combed neatly by whoever had put on the bandage, but the ash-blonde colour made her look even more pallid.

All Leah wanted was for Ash to open her eyes and smile at her.

"Can you leave me to sit with her for a while, please?" she asked without turning away from Ashley.

Taking her friend's limp, uninjured hand in hers, she waited to hear if her wishes would be honoured. She only wanted time alone with Ashley, to take in all that had happened to them since leaving their base ship on this exploration mission.

"All right," said Darius, "we will leave you alone for a little while but if she awakens or you become concerned, just call out. I will leave one of my men outside the room in case you need anything."

Moments later she heard the soft snick of the closing door.

Relief washed over Leah. At last she could relax without being under scrutiny. It was unsettling to be in close proximity to someone whose very presence made her body react in the way it did. She still felt tingles on her skin from where he had touched her as he carried her here.

Not even Jason, her intended mate, had that spine-tingling effect on her. With a single look Darius affected her more than making love to Jason had.

She shuddered to think of what Jason must be feeling now, knowing she was long overdue to report in their findings. The last time she had seen him had been just before she and Ashley left on what was to be their last mission. After that they would settle down with their mates and produce their quota of offspring for the next generation. At least it was not all duty for Ashley; she had known her intended mate since childhood.

Although mated at birth by proxy, she and Jason had only met six months ago, when he had joined her base ship as part of the exchange of females and males from other communities. The exchange served as a balance so that the genetics of her people would not grow stale. It was a good idea and also necessary, but it was hard not to have enough time to learn more about each other's habits… and faults.

At least her commander, her father, had listened to her pleas to be allowed more time to become familiar with her intended before settling down to mated life. In fact, it was only in the last month that their relationship had progressed to a more intimate stage at Jason's instigation. She would have been pleased to wait until they were officially joined, but it was the only way she could get his agreement to go on this, her last assignment.

The joining had served one purpose. She now knew that sexually there would be no tingles or sparks. They would have a comfortable relationship. She could spend her days in such a relationship. Couldn't she? The fire that Darius had made her feel flared through her again, but she fought it down.

As she sat listening to Ashley's breathing, she thought about her last encounter with Jason, the night before they left on this mission.

* * *

Darius was glad he did not have to explain immediately to his irate mate the ramifications of her landing on his world. She had enough to cope with this night and tomorrow would be soon enough. The explanation was not something he was looking forward to, as he had no doubt she would not like what he had to tell her. At least while she was occupied with her friend he could catch up on pack business.

"How are the preparations going for the joining ceremony, Mata?" he asked as he waited for Kell, his second-in-command, to join them.

"All is well. Our people are so happy to do this for you that they are working hard to make sure everything is completed for tomorrow."

"Good. I want everything ready for mid-day. I will not wait any longer to claim my mate." Darius looked up as the door opened and Kell walked into the room. One look told Darius that Kell was agitated.

"Jageri have been spotted near our borders. I have sent a group to investigate the number, but from what our scout said, it was at least fifty males of their pack."

"Mata! What do you know of this?" said Darius, turning toward his Seer. He saw that she was communicating with someone and did not appear too pleased with what she was learning.

"That was Jilla, the Jageri Seer; she is with the group that approaches. Darius, you have to let them through. They come for their leader's life mate," Mata answered, in a hesitant voice.

"Ashley is the mate of Jarod of the Jageri?" Darius stood to pace. "I could do without this at the moment. I have not claimed my own mate and now I will have to tell her that her friend will be leaving her new home! She will not be pleased."

Although he wondered what he could do to make this easier on both of the females, he knew the law had to be followed, no matter the cost in personal sacrifice. He could only hope that the Jageri leader would take their mates' friendship into consideration and allow them to meet at regular intervals. Stopping his pacing to consider this, he decided that he would be willing to call truce if the Jageri would do the same. Darius believed once Jarod had his mate, he would do anything to keep her content and happy. All men found out quickly that an unhappy mate was not easy to live with.

"Mata, inform Jilla that the Jageri are to wait on our borders till Kell arrives to escort them to our stronghold. But tell her that only she, Jarod and six others are being given safe passage. All others must wait on their side of the border. Our pack will stand guard to make sure these instructions are followed. That is my word on safe passage for mate claiming."

Darius turned from Mata to Kell, knowing she would follow his orders to the letter. "Take your men and escort our guests. Tell them they will be witness to my joining." Sighing, Darius watched his friend leave the room after acknowledging his orders.

He crossed to a table and poured himself a large measure from the carafe of wine sitting there. Drinking down the contents of the glass in one go, he waited for Mata to finish her communication.

"They are not happy with the amount of men you are allowing over the border. But they recognise your vow of safe passage, and will stay at the border till Kell arrives to escort them here. I must go and see that preparations are made for the Jageri party. I will leave you to make sure your mate does not stay with her friend for much longer. She needs her rest," Mata said as she moved toward the door.

Darius walked to his favourite chair and sat, enjoying the warmth from the fire. His thoughts turned toward his mate and, without intending to, linked with her. Skilfully keeping himself in the back of her mind, hidden from her awareness, he probed her. The thoughts running through her mind enraged him.

Chapter Four

"Jason, you gave me a fright. I thought we had already said our goodbyes."

"I could not let you leave without holding you one more time, Leah," he said, pulling her closer to him. He covered her mouth with his.

As his tongue stroked hers, she became aroused by his kiss. He moved his hand to the zipper of her uniform and pulled it down slowly, releasing her full breasts to his touch. Her nipples turned to hard kernels as he sucked each in turn.

With great patience, he pulled her uniform to her waist then let it slide past her hips. He knelt and pulled it down the rest of the way, gently lifting one leg at a time to remove it altogether. Remaining on his knees, he waited for Leah to open her legs a bit wider so that he had better access to her pussy. Jason pulled open her labia, licking as far as his tongue would go. Pulling his head closer, not caring if he had difficulty breathing, she moved nearer to orgasm. Swirls of tension filled her with pleasure, and she wanted to enjoy every moment before she had to leave…

Darius pulled himself from Leah's thoughts with a roar, tightening his grip on his wine glass and breaking it with the force of his feelings.

"How dare she think of another man? She is *my* mate." Jumping up, uncaring that his hand bled from the broken glass, he strode toward the door, nearly knocking Mata down as she entered.

"What is the matter? Your hand is bleeding. Let me take care of it for you," she said, concern sounding in her voice. "How did you do this?"

"I am going to prove to my mate that I am the only man she needs in her life! Let me be," he growled, trying to brush past her. But she held on to his arm. He had too much respect for her to force her aside.

"What did you mean by that? Have you been in her thoughts?"

"It was unintentional. She was thinking of another male making love to her! Why would she think of another when I am here?" In the back of his mind, he knew it was unreasonable to feel betrayal. Leah didn't yet understand that they were intended only for each other. Well, by all that he held sacred he swore that it would be the last damned time another man clouded her thoughts!

Mata used her healing energy on his wound, closing it until it looked like a week-old cut, not a newly made one. Darius grunted his thanks.

"I am going to claim my mate! She will see that I am all she needs or wants." Darius stormed through the open doorway before she could say anything else to him.

Mata hurried to catch up to him before he could burst into the room where his mate watched over her injured friend.

* * *

Leah jumped to her feet as the door crashed against the wall. Startled, her hand flew to her throat and she stared at Darius standing in the doorway. She might have only met him that day but she could tell he was furious. The harsh sound of his breath was the only sound in the room. His chest heaved as if he had just run a great distance.

"What is wrong? Why are you looking at me like that?" she said in a confused voice.

Darius moved further into the room, closing the gap until he towered over her. He sniffed the air about them as he drew closer. Whatever scent he picked up, he did not like it. His eyes were angry slits as he closed in on her.

He backed Leah up against the pallet, leaving her no room to escape. His bunched muscles and angry expression warned her of his dangerous mood. Adrenaline coursed through her body as her eyes scanned the room for anything she might use to defend herself.

"You're coming with me." His voice was too low, too calm. He grabbed her arm and pulled her toward the door.

Leah tried to yank her arm free from his punishing grip. But Darius was unrelenting as he dragged her through the doorway.

"You can't just drag me around like this!" Leah was indignant.

He turned to glare at her. Good, she thought, she could reason with him. But before she could say anything else he grabbed her about the waist and hauled her over his right shoulder, continuing on his way.

Humiliated that his people could see how he was treating her as they passed, she pummelled his unyielding back with every ounce of her strength. The muscles on his buttocks tightened with each step he took, catching her eye. Why she noticed that now, in her anger, she didn't know.

He entered a room that appeared to be the one she had been in earlier. He crossed toward the sleeping pallet and laid her down on it, surprisingly gentle, considering how angry he was. Leah shot up on the pallet but he was on her in an instant, his hand between her breasts to stop her from moving.

"Let me sit up! What is wrong with you?"

His eyes searched hers and her breath caught in her throat as she noticed that his eyes were glowing again, flickering from his normal deep blue to a silvery glow and back.

"Why were you thinking of making love to another male when you are my mate?" he demanded through gritted teeth.

Leah felt warmth flood her face. But wait! The only way he could know she had been thinking of her last night with Jason was if he could read her thoughts. She felt violated. How *could* he do something like that to her?

"How did you know what I had been thinking?" she asked him, trying again to sit up. "How could you read my thoughts?"

"You are my mate; we can communicate that way, but that is not what I asked. Why, when I am here, did you think of making love to another?"

He undid the fastenings on the bodice of her tunic as he spoke, ignoring her attempts to stop him. Her nipples tightened under his intense gaze. A shiver ran down her spine as he took one between his thumb and forefinger and pinched it lightly.

"Stop that, Darius. We have to talk about this." She tried to brush his hand away. But he paid no attention, lowering his mouth to close over the nipple nearest to him. His amazing tongue flicked over the tip. The rough texture of it felt so much better now she was awake to enjoy it. The abrasiveness rasped over the sensitive point sending shudders of pleasure down through her body. *She should not be allowing this to happen.*

Darius looked up at her, his eyes shining in the darkened room. She did not feel afraid, knowing somehow he would never hurt her.

He looked away from her face and down her body, his hands pulling the tunic from her before sliding back up toward her pussy. Leah clamped her legs together but he pulled them apart easily, his fingers delving through the blonde curls at the top of her thighs toward her hot, wet centre.

"You are wet. You want me as much as I want you. Do not try to tell me different." He brought his wet fingers to his nose and sniffed, then put them in his mouth and licked her juices from them, closing his eyes as though savouring the taste of her.

Leah blushed all over. She couldn't help making comparisons. Jason had never made her feel this way. Just watching Darius enjoying her taste excited her more than a full-blown orgasm with her intended mate.

She wanted him to touch her again, to feel the caress of his fingers, his mouth and more. Although she didn't want these feelings, they were real and she could not ignore them, not when she felt his hard cock pressing into her hip. She knew she should stop him, but the way he was stroking her clit, she did not have the will.

She had to be honest with herself. She wanted him to continue.

"I should not feel this way about you. I am promised to one of my people. Why do you affect me this way?" She examined his beautiful deep blue eyes, eyes that slanted upwards slightly at the corner. Funny she hadn't noticed that before. But now she was so close to him his eyes were all she could see. His scent was driving her mad, making her do and feel things that she otherwise would not do.

She moved her hand over his erection, touching it gently. He looked into her eyes, watching as she licked her lips. His cock jumped in her hand and she gave an answering squeeze.

"Why do you say I am your mate? How can you know something like that? You don't know me." All the while, she stroked her fingers up and down his cock, feeling it lengthen and thicken… if that was possible. It had seemed impossibly big before.

"The Seers of our people have pre-cognitive dreams. I knew you were my mate before you arrived here. Mata saw your arrival on our world."

His breath caught in his throat as her hand moved to undo the fastening of his loincloth. She noticed the wet spot from his pre-ejaculate.

He put his hand gently on hers. "If you don't want this to continue tonight, then now is the time to stop. Any more of that and we take this to the finish."

Now that she was the one to make the decision to continue with this lovemaking, Leah didn't know what to do. When he had been in control she had an excuse to let it continue. Suddenly she was assailed with doubts. She thought of Jason and what he and the rest of her people would think if they found out. Did she want Darius more than she wanted to keep faith with her people?

Darius watched her closely, knowing from her frown that she was having second thoughts about continuing. He bowed his head, knowing he had given her the choice, and he would honour it… at least tonight.

He moved his fingers away from her pussy and licked them clean, all the time watching her eyes, seeing them cloud with passion once more. Her hand still encircled his cock, but now he removed it and stood up carefully, trying not to groan in pain. He was steel hard but there was no relief in sight this evening.

"I will make sure refreshments are sent to you. I will see you tomorrow for our joining," he said as he walked quickly toward the door.

"Wait, what do you mean *joining*?"

He faced her. "You are my mate, Leah. Our people are preparing for our joining ceremony tomorrow. Sleep well and I will see you then." He turned once more and left the room just before he heard her shriek. Chuckling to himself, he caught sight of Mata waiting in the corridor.

"Make sure my mate has food and that she rests for tomorrow. I am going to hunt. I need to run to clear my head." He headed toward the doorway to the courtyard.

Once he was outside, his body started to contort and change. His arms and hands morphed into legs and paws. Once his change was completed, a large black cat stood where Darius had. Sleek and powerful, the predator looked forward to his hunt tonight, as he needed a kill to calm himself down.

Chapter Five

Mata walked into the room as Leah stood fastening the tunic she had been wearing earlier. The woman's presence pulled Leah from her thoughts of tracking Darius down and demanding an explanation from him.

"I have come to take you to the bathing pool. It will make you feel better." Mata motioned toward the fastenings Leah struggled with. "Let me help you with this. It takes some time to get used to the clips on these tunics."

"Did you see Darius? I must talk to him." She remained still while Mata helped.

"He will be back later. Some important things have to be taken care of that only he can deal with." Mata gently took Leah's arm and led her to the door. "After you have bathed and eaten you will feel much more relaxed. Come, it is not far."

Walking down the corridor, Leah tried not to make eye contact with any of the people walking about. She was so embarrassed that they might have seen her slung over Darius's shoulder.

Mata opened one of the many doors before them and led her into a warm room with a centrally placed pool that took up most of the available space. Leah watched Mata move to one of the benches that ran along the wall and remove her tunic before walking carefully down into the pool. Leah followed her actions and joined her in the warm soothing water.

"This is the female bathing area. The communal one is a few doors down but I thought you would prefer the of the different Leopai pack leaders are travelling to witness your joining tomorrow; it is a cause for celebration as Darius is the leader of the Leopai cousin lines." Mata stood and left the pool, making her way to where the drying cloths were hanging.

Leah did not know how to respond to that news. Darius was not just the leader of this pack but over others? What would that make her if she were his mate? Deciding to keep her thoughts to herself for the present, she rose from the tub and joined Mata in drying herself.

She put on the clean tunic Mata gave her to wear. She followed her to another room and settled down to have something to eat. Leah noticed the room had large tables set in a U-shape in front of the main table. She thought this must be a central dining room, as she noticed that there were both males and females eating. Older females served food and drink when they were seated.

"Tomorrow I will make you a restorative drink," Mata said as they finished eating. "I will have it sent to your room with your breakfast. It is important that you drink it all, as it will help you keep up your stamina for the joining ceremony."

"I am not Darius's mate, no matter that you think I am. My people never mate with other species, it is against our laws. I am sorry but it will not happen."

"The signs are never wrong. You *are* his mate. Tell me, is it normal for your people to react as you do? With a male of another species?" Mata grinned as though she knew the answer. "You have to admit that you feel something for Darius. Sorry to be blunt, but I can smell the scent of your arousal when he is near you."

Feeling her face heat, Leah acknowledged what Mata said was true. As much as she wished she could deny it, *yes,* she did grow aroused whenever she was near Darius. And it was so unlike her to feel strongly about someone she had just met, she didn't know how to handle the situation.

Well, she could go on arguing with Mata, but she wanted to know more about Darius, about the kind of man he was. For some reason she did not think Mata would be forthcoming. Mata had decided that Leah was her leader's mate and so nothing else needed to be said. But she had the feeling there was more to this group, or *pack* as they referred to themselves, than they were telling.

"You look exhausted, Leah. Come. It is time you rested. There is tomorrow to discuss things. The ceremony takes place at mid-day and there will be preparations in the morning when we can talk. For now it is time you were asleep."

"I need you to tell me more about this mating ceremony. There is no way I am going through that no matter what you believe. But I would like to know something about it anyway," said Leah, trying not to be overheard by the others in the room. She was drawing enough attention to herself by being a stranger and being so physically different from these tall dark-haired people.

"It is a joining for life between you and Darius. You will be mated in front of the pack so that they can witness your joining."

"What do you mean, mated in front of the pack?" Leah asked, although from the phrasing that Mata used she had a good idea, and there was no way *that* was going to happen. She was not letting Darius fuck her in front of his pack or anyone else for that matter. Was that how he got his kicks?

"Our Shaman will join you both in a ceremony. He will make a cut on the palm of your hands and join them together to mingle your blood. Darius will then mate with you, with us as witness. It is a very beautiful ceremony. There is nothing to be afraid of and you will not be harmed. But you need to be presented to our people so that they can see for themselves the mother of our next pack leader. Not just our pack but the cousin lines as well. The alphas must be shown that the next leader will be as strong as Darius, and capable of leadership. They need to know that you are strong enough to carry and nurture his heir."

Leah's face flushed and her hands clenched into fists as she heard this. "My getting fucked in front of them will tell them I am strong enough to bear an alpha to lead them? Come on. Don't expect me to believe that for one minute. This is just so you can play voyeur. I will not be a part of this! I want to be taken to the shuttle tomorrow so I can try and repair the communications panel to contact my people." Leah stood up and headed toward the door. "This conversation is closed, and I will take your advice and go to sleep. I will have a busy day tomorrow fixing things on our shuttle."

When Mata joined her outside the dining room, Leah noticed the sceptical glance that she gave her. Up until now she had gone along with what they said, first because she had ached all over from the crash, and then concern for Ashley had put a stop to any immediate thoughts of returning to the shuttle. But after the conversation she had just had with Mata, returning to the shuttle was the most important thing she could do now. She *had* to contact her people.

Chapter Six

Darius entered the compound after his mind-clearing run, thankful that he had managed to get his emotions under control. He was aware of the Jageri scent in his territory. Had been since he reached the boundary of the hunting grounds, but knew that there was nothing he could do but accept their presence. That did nothing to set his mind at ease, not when his unclaimed mate was now here. Her protection was the most important thing to him. His only option was to sleep in the room with her, to protect her as a mate should.

He stayed in his feline form and padded through the doorway, lightly touching the minds of his men guarding it. As he made his way to his private quarters, Kell filled him in on the Jageri situation. Grateful that there was nothing more for him to do this night, he made his way to Leah. A guard was in his place outside the door and opened it for him. Once inside, he made his way toward the pallet and his sleeping mate.

Sitting and resting his head beside Leah's arm, he rubbed his nose over her skin, wanting to leave a trail of his scent on her to warn any other male that she belonged to him. She had bathed while he was hunting; he smelled the gentle scent of lavender under her unique fragrance. Ah, no other female smelled quite like her. Standing, he walked to the hearth still warmed by the fire now dying in the grate. Making sure he could easily see both the door and balcony off the room, as well as Leah, he lay down. It was going to be a long night.

Darius was startled from his light sleep. Dazed, he searched the darkness for the disturbance. Looking at Leah, he saw her move restlessly on the pallet, twisting the covers down to her waist and giving him a view of her beautiful breasts. Making his way soundlessly to her, he settled down with his head once more within touching distance of her hand and gently entered her mind to see what had disturbed her sleep.

Leah gripped his long, thick cock, moving her hand up and down the length. Leaning closer she licked the drop of pre-come from the end of the ruddy-looking head, then opened her mouth to take in the first inch. Moving her tongue around the tip, she made sure she tasted all the drops that leaked into her mouth. Moving her head backwards and forwards, she took more of his cock into her mouth.

Darius looked down at Leah kneeling in front of him, sucking as much of his cock into her mouth as she was able to take. He cradled her face, gently guided her in a rhythm that brought him pleasure. Leah groaned her enjoyment as she worked on him, and he growled in response, his cock growing even longer with her ministrations.

Taking one hand off him, she touched his testicles. With growing excitement, she rubbed the base with care, then ran her finger along the skin of his scrotum toward his anal opening and back.

Leah looked up at Darius. His face had already flushed with excitement at her actions, but she wanted to make it even better for him.

"Lie down. I want to be able to touch all of you." Moving back and smiling at him, she stood and took his hand to lead him to the pallet. Waiting until he did as she requested, she straddled him and lowered her head to kiss his sensual mouth. Searching for his tongue, she touched it with hers, and they explored each other's taste. With reluctance she left his mouth to kiss her way down his

throat to his small hard nipples. Was he as sensitive as she was there? She had to find out.

Taking one in her mouth Leah sucked on the tip, moving from one to the other until she heard him groan. Planting kisses down his firm, toned stomach, she headed for her goal, his thick, hard and weeping cock. This was what she wanted to suck on.

The velvety hard shaft lengthened in her hand. She guided the tip into her mouth with a moan of appreciation at the delicious taste. She licked around the head, bathing his cock from tip to base.

"Turn around and lie on me, Leah. I want to lick your pussy while you suck my cock," he growled.

Although she did not want to stop her exploration of his cock, she wanted to feel his tongue in her wet pussy, so she turned around and moved backwards until he gripped her hips, bringing her swollen labia nearer his face. She felt his breath on her protruding clit then the touch of his tongue.

Once again taking his cock into her mouth, she sucked harder in response to his tongue entering the hot, wet heart of her pussy. She moaned in total pleasure at the feel of it, moving in and out deep within her.

Although enjoyable, this was not how either of them wanted to climax. Lifting herself, Leah reluctantly moved away from Darius's talented tongue and turned around to face him once more. Moving her pussy in line with his cock, she lowered herself onto his hard length, using her hand to guide him, only managing to take an inch at a time. She had to go slowly as he was so thick she felt stretched and full.

After what seemed like an eternity, her wet labia met the base of his cock, and she shuddered at the delicious feeling of fullness inside her pussy. Moving, she lifted herself up and down, slowly, feeling Darius's stomach muscles contract with her movements. She picked up speed as she felt a pressure beginning to start in the very centre of her being.

Darius squeezed her breasts, moving his fingers to her taut nipples and pinching them hard. The pleasure-pain she felt made her move even faster on his cock. Lifting his head he took one of her distended nipples into his mouth and sucked strongly, then left a trail of moisture as he moved to the other and repeated his actions.

Leaving her breasts, he gripped her hips to help her move faster and faster as he pushed upwards in time with her rhythm, until they let out moans of release as they reached fulfilment. With her pussy still pulsing in time with his cock, she collapsed onto his chest. Tired but satisfied, she drifted to sleep in his arms.

Darius pulled himself from her thoughts, growling as his cock spurted his release over the fur covering his belly and chest.

She began to waken, either from his growl or from her dream. He didn't want her to know he was in her room, even though it was for her protection. Silently and swiftly he moved into the shadows of the room, away from the glow of the fire.

* * *

Coming slowly awake, she lay still and remembered. An erotic encounter was not something Leah dreamed about very often... at least not one as explicit as this one. She could have sworn she had actually heard Darius's growl of satisfaction at his orgasm and could smell his unique scent in the room. She shouldn't be surprised that he played a part in the dream, considering their last encounter... and the discussion she had with Mata after he made his oh-so-annoying exit.

Hearing a noise in the corridor outside the door broke into Leah's recollections of last evening's encounter with Mata. All that had come of it was that Darius was firmly fixed in her mind when she tried to sleep, which must have been the reason for the dream she had. He was all she could think of.

It was still the middle of the night. There would be time later to think of ways she could get out of this predicament. She needed sleep to figure out a way to communicate with her people so they could rescue Ashley and herself.

* * *

Waking to the sound of the door being opened, Leah managed to stop herself from gasping at the sight that met her eyes. A large black cat with a compact, muscular body, about seven and a half feet in length, exited through the open doorway. Keeping still until the door was closed, Leah shivered in reaction to the thought that a predator had been in her room. *How did it get in?*

Glancing out the window, she noticed that it was close to dawn. Now would be a good time to try to return to the shuttle and see what could be done to fix the communications panel. She wasn't going to lie here waiting until Mata came in and started going on about "mating ceremonies" again.

Rising from the sleeping pallet and putting on the tunic that she had worn the night before, she tiptoed to the doors of the balcony and carefully opened them. Thankfully there was no one in sight as she moved to the wall of the balcony to swing her legs over the side and lower herself down to the ground.

Hoping she remembered the way back to the shuttle, she knew this would likely be the only chance she would have. Checking to see where the sun was rising, she calculated the direction the shuttle had crashed. Remembering where the sun had been in the sky when she had been brought to Darius's home, she set off in that direction.

Leah couldn't believe that she had managed to get so far undetected. There had been no one she'd been forced to hide from. All she could see from a distance were large black cats that seemed to be looking for prey of a different sort. But she kept a wary eye on them just the same. At last spotting the gleam of metal shimmering in the growing light from the sun, Leah let out a relieved sigh that she had made it back to the shuttle without any mishap.

"Well, this will never fly again," Leah muttered as she looked over the damage the crash had made to the exterior of the shuttle. Moving to the hatch, she pulled herself up through the opening and carefully stood, looking around at the devastation of the interior. She headed for the communications panel, careful not to stand on anything lying around the floor as she might have to salvage some of it for repairs. Knowing it was hopeless, she still tried to use the communication device, but she heard nothing. Not even static. *This looks like it will take a while to fix, if I can fix it at all.* Moving toward the compartment that held the repair tools, she settled down to make major repairs.

This is hopeless, Leah thought an hour later. *I just don't have the tools for repairing this amount of damage*. Looking at the wires she had been reattaching to the panel, she knew that it was beyond her abilities to fix. They were stuck here unless Ashley could devise a way to strip other panels of materials to use on the communicator.

Wait, there should be a signal beacon on board. Why hadn't she thought about this yesterday? Well, she reminded herself, there were her own injuries and wanting to care for Ashley's. She sighed at the vision of her friend as she had been last night, lying pale and helpless on her pallet. Now, for both their sakes, Leah had to concentrate on the task at hand.

She headed for the compartments at the rear of the shuttle where the mobile beacon should be. When she arrived, the cabinet stood open, the contents of the compartment scattered around the floor, just like so many other instruments.

If only she could get a signal to her people. Their base ship knew their last coordinates; it wouldn't take much for them to realise this was the only place they could have crashed.

Leah knew it was going to be difficult to evade any search parties that Darius had sent after her once he realised she was missing. But she would not give up her freedom of choice for anyone. Not even a man who made her pussy wet just by looking at her. Sex wasn't everything. She needed to feel wanted for herself and that took time. Regardless of how he made her feel, she did not know Darius. No matter how he affected her physically she was not prepared to go along with his demands just because he said so. *I need a much better reason than that.*

A noise outside the shuttle alerted her to the fact that she had been found. Deciding that the best way to handle this was to be assertive and take the fight to Darius, she headed to the opening. Only, the sight that met her eyes was not the one she was expecting.

Moving around the outside of the shuttle were two large cats, slightly larger than the black one she had seen in her room. These were a brownish/yellow colour with dark rosette markings; they were more muscular and stocky than the black one had been. Why she noticed all this in her surprise she couldn't tell, but she did. The cats looked up, sniffing the air as they did.

She couldn't hide her gasp of shock at what happened next. The cats looked at each other then their bodies convulsed. Legs and paws changed into legs, arms and hands; their bodies morphed into tall, muscular men. Their dark blond hair showed golden streaks running through it. The men were identical in every way, except one of them had a scar on the right side of his face. Leah felt her legs give way and she sat down hard on her bottom as she wondered, not for the first time, just what kind of planet this was.

Chapter Seven

The scene that met Darius made him growl with rage. First he'd heard from his men that Leah was attempting to return to the shuttle. He allowed it because he wanted to let her see for herself that there was nothing she could do to contact her people. Besides, she was safe with his men following to keep her from harm. But when he received word that two of the Jageri had left the compound to go to the hunting grounds where the shuttle crashed, he was furious. At her for wanting to leave and at himself for letting her have the freedom to try. Her reaction to the morphing of Jarod and his twin brother Jeran was as he feared it would be… overwhelming to her. He would rather have shown her himself when he could explain and help her understand.

Darius growled instructions to his men in mind talk, and they all came out of the trees to surround the shuttle and the two Jageri. Darius snarled a challenge to the two muscular men standing between him and his mate, letting them know he would fight to reach her if they foolishly tried to stop him. Watching them move aside, he walked purposefully toward the opening of the shuttle.

Looking upwards at his mate, he kept his gaze fixed on her. Slowly he changed into his human self. She gasped and became paler. He willed her not to break his gaze, but she covered her face with her hands. His heart skipped a beat as he watched them tremble. When she looked up and shook her head in disbelief, he knew the rest of his men had changed too, a fact he confirmed when he touched Kell's mind.

"Come down from there, Leah. It is time to return to the compound," he growled at her. He should have been gentler because she had to be in shock from what she had witnessed. But his anger with her hadn't left him.

Leah stared at him as though she couldn't believe what she was hearing or seeing.

"We would not have harmed your mate, Darius." Jarod moved to stand beside him. "We picked up her scent and came to investigate what she was doing here. We thought you would have had her safely tucked up in your quarters."

"I hope our mate will not be so reckless with her behaviour," said Jeran, walking to his brother's side.

"Our mate?" Darius turned to face them. "She is to be mate to you both?"

"Did Jilla not pass that news to Mata? We thought she would have when she informed you of our presence on your lands. We do everything together. She will be well protected with both of us watching over her," Jarod said, glancing up at a stunned-looking Leah.

"Who are they talking about, Darius? Who is their mate?" Leah asked in a shaky voice.

Darius moved toward her till he could just about touch her legs. She jerked them away before he could.

"Come down, Leah. Let me help you." Darius tried not to frighten her any further. He could see she was having difficulty understanding all that was happening. When he reached up again, she let him put his hands on her waist and lower her to the ground.

"Tell me who they were talking about! Who is their mate?"

"I can answer that for you," said Jarod. "Your companion is our mate. When she awakens we will claim her as ours."

Leah swung her head back toward Darius and he nodded in agreement.

"Ashley will never agree to that, just as I am not agreeing to mate with Darius, so I wouldn't bother waiting for her to wake up." Leah looked from one identical face to the other.

"Leah, it is not up for discussion. You are my mate just as Ashley is the mate of Jarod and Jeran."

"Who on Skyla are you two anyway?" Leah asked Jarod. "You are not like Darius and the rest of his... What are you?" Leah asked, turning back to Darius.

Darius turned toward the two Jageri, wanting to pound them into the ground for springing this revelation on his mate without giving him time to prepare her. If he had to deal with them right now he knew he would start a fight, and then be accused of breaking mate law. Letting Kell know through mind talk that the twins were his responsibility, he turned back to face his mate.

"I think it is time to return to the compound. You are not used to the weather conditions here yet and the heat will soon become unpleasant for you." Darius took her arm in his and led her away from the shuttle and back to the compound. He ignored her attempts to question him; he would ask Mata to tell her more about his pack later.

* * *

Leah watched Darius out of the corner of her eye as they returned to the compound. She was angry with him for keeping so many secrets from her, for not explaining how he and the rest of his people could change form. And who were those two men? They weren't Darius's people. That was obvious from the different colour and animal they appeared to be when in cat form. In fact from what she had observed, they were definitely not on friendly terms.

She knew she had to calm herself. One part of her wanted to scream at Darius for trying to take over her life, and the other wanted to melt in his arms at the masterful way he stated that she belonged to him.

Although she didn't want to go against her teachings, she had a feeling that for her own personal happiness, she had to find out what was running through Darius's mind. And what was that he told her last evening? That on this world mates had a mind link with each other. What she felt about that she wasn't sure right now, but she needed to find out things that Darius was reluctant to tell her.

She reached out with her mind toward Darius, being careful not to arouse his defences by being as clumsy as she had been yesterday. She'd been as subtle as a brick in her haste to try and get away from his disconcerting touch at the crash site and last night when she woke up.

Entering his mind was like walking through thick fog, trying to see a landmark so you knew where you were. Now, knowing that his brain patterns were so different from what she was used to dealing with, she knew that if she sensed anything out of the ordinary that would be the key to entering his memories.

Leah stumbled on the uneven ground. Darius growled just before he swept her off her feet and cradled her in his arms, continuing on his way to the compound without breaking his stride. She felt his arms tighten about her body when she tried to make herself a bit more comfortable.

"Settle down, I won't drop you," Darius told her in a husky voice.

Leah felt her pussy flood with moisture in reaction to the sound of his voice. At least now she didn't have to concentrate on her movements. Closing her eyes, she returned her attention to her task of gathering information.

There! She had never seen anything like that little silver light. Approaching it carefully Leah stepped through the transparent barrier that kept her from entering Darius's mind. It was like coming out of a dark forest into a bright sunny day.

Now that she was in known territory, she released the breath she had been holding. Opening her eyes, she checked to make sure that Darius wasn't aware of her intrusion. His attention was fixed on the path before them, so she felt safe enough returning to her explorations.

The first thing she discovered caused her to draw in her breath sharply.

Darius was in tremendous pain! Pain that seemed to be caused by the proximity of… Herself? Yes! She was the one causing him pain. How could he bear it? How was she the cause of it? She had to find out. Moving further into the light, she started sifting through his newest memories, trying to learn what she needed to know.

Tears gathered behind her eyelids at what she found. She was the cause of his pain because she was his mate. There was no doubt in Darius's mind or his body's reactions to being near her. A mate was normally claimed when they met, but Darius had given her time to get to know him before he made his direct claim.

If she refused to mate with Darius, he believed in his heart that he would never have children of his own. Only true mates had any hope of having children together.

But what caused her tears was the overpowering emotion that poured from him toward her. He didn't just feel sexual attraction toward her, as she had thought. He was growing to care for her as a person and not simply because she was his biological mate.

Leah pulled free from his memories. She opened her eyes and looked into Darius's face. He must have felt her stare because he took his eyes from the path and returned her gaze.

"We shall be at the compound soon. I will take you to Mata. She will take you to bathe and get something to eat before the ceremony."

"No, Darius. We have to talk first. Don't look at me like that," she said, watching his eyebrows draw together as he frowned down at her. "This is too important to both of us. You have to answer my questions. I want to know things only you can tell me."

Leah hoped she was getting through to him. They had to talk now! Now, before things went any further.

She reached up and touched the side of his face. He sucked in his breath and she felt the shudder that ran through his body at her touch.

The way he reacts to me will take some getting used to. His eyes began to glow, and she realised now that this was a sign of his arousal.

He turned his face into her hand to place a kiss on her palm, making her feel cared for. That was what had been missing with Jason, the mate chosen for her by her people. He'd never once made her feel she was needed. She was only a duty to him. There had always been something missing, but she hadn't known what until she felt the need running through every touch Darius had given her.

Tenderness wrenched her heart as she watched him nuzzle her hand. Then he lifted his head and looked into her eyes. What he looked for she didn't know, but he must have seen something there that convinced him that she was serious in what she said.

"Very well, we will talk when we arrive back home," he said with a sigh as he turned toward Kell. She could only presume that he was giving Kell instructions using mind talk.

The rest of the journey was made in silence until they arrived at the compound. Darius nodded to his men standing guard at the doorway to the inner courtyard then he carried her down the long corridor to his personal rooms.

Chapter Eight

Darius shut the door behind them. Leaning against it with eyes closed, he took a deep breath, inhaling Leah's scent. He opened his eyes and looked down at his mate, held in the cradle of his arms. He knew she would not believe the pleasure it gave him to hold her close like this. Or the pain he felt.

The pain in his head alone was becoming harder to bear, but it was his choice to wait to claim Leah. She deserved a chance to know him better. If she were Catarian he would have linked with her right away, because she would have known the effects of not doing so, how it would affect both of them. But Leah was not of Catari. He had tried to limit the time spent alone with his mate and had avoided her questions when he could, but the look in her eyes on the journey home had made him realise that she deserved to know the truth.

But what was the truth? Did he want her to know the effect she had on him? The way his body tightened every time he was in scenting distance of her? Even when he wasn't in the actual room with her, he knew the delicious scent that was so unique to his mate. He had tried to protect himself by ignoring her questions, but that was at an end now.

He removed his arm from under her legs and let Leah slide down his body to the floor. He was so hard he knew she had to feel the evidence of his erection against her belly as she stood close against him. Darius watched a blush form on her face and neck.

"What do you want to know first?" he asked, keeping her close to him by leaving his hands on her waist.

Leah cleared her throat and looked away from his gaze. She took a step back and he released his grip, though it was the last thing he wanted to do.

"Tell me what it means to be a life mate. What do you feel for me?" She backed away from him.

Darius watched as Leah retreated into the middle of his room, standing beside one of his lounging chairs. His chest tightened with pain, knowing she didn't want to be near him, but what could he expect? What could he tell her to explain his need? What should he tell her first?

"When a Catari male first encounters his mate, both of them realise right away they are mates, and it is instinctual to want to link minds with each other. Even if the actual physical joining is delayed, the mind link is normally immediate. But you are not of Catari. I didn't want you to feel overwhelmed yesterday so I never attempted to mate link with you. I wanted you to learn something about my people first." He searched her face to gauge her reaction. Darius wanted to say the right things to her. She needed to know more, but in words that she would understand and not reject out of hand.

"Then why did you not answer my questions last night? Why leave it to Mata to try and explain some of the ceremony? I would have thought that would be a good chance for us to get to know each other better." Leah sat, but on the edge of the chair, as though wanting to make a quick escape.

Darius knew he could not hide anything more from her; she would have to learn everything now. Stepping away from the door, he moved nearer his mate and sat opposite her. Within touching distance if she wanted to touch him, but far enough away so he hoped she didn't feel pressured by his presence. He had heard stories of suffering with flashing lights and blurred vision when the link was not put into place quickly enough. He hoped he could explain things before it was too unbearable to be in the same room as Leah.

"It is painful for me to be near you and not have a link with you. You are the other half of my soul, the one I have been waiting for my whole life. I need to link with you, to join our minds. It would have been unfair for me to do this without your consent. I could not force this on you, even though it was my first and second thought to do just that."

Darius met her gaze as she looked up at his words. What was that look she had? It was as if she understood his pain! But how was that possible?

"Why do your people need a mind link with your mates? How can this be so important to you?"

"It is important as it keeps the males grounded. We are a race of predators, and our mates keep us from going wild. It is hard enough when we are alone, but when a mate enters our lives nothing and no one can be allowed to harm her. We need to touch the minds of our mates once we meet them. To not have this is unsettling to a Catarian. Once the link is in place we would be aware of each other all the time. You would just have to think of me and you would know where I was and what I was doing. But you have to open yourself up to me, to allow me in; I cannot force you to do that."

He watched her reaction. Would he have to tell her that the Shaman had enough power to dull her senses so that Darius could put the link in place without her consent? No! That might be better kept to himself for now. Theirs was a fragile relationship and he needed and wanted her agreement to the joining.

"If I agreed to link with you, if we joined and it didn't work out or my people came for me… What would you do if I wanted to leave with them?"

Troubled, Darius looked into her eyes. A knot tightened in his chest at the mention of her people. He would never give her up once she joined with him. It was unthinkable.

"Once we join, we will be as one. It will 'work out,' as you put it. Have no fear of that, little one." He took her hand in his and kissed her palm. He felt the shudder that ran along her arm at his kiss and from the smouldering fire burning in her eyes he knew it was not in rejection of his touch, but acceptance. The scent of her arousal wafted up at him and he inhaled deeply, closing his eyes to prevent her from seeing the full strength of his hunger for her. He wondered if this would work out after all.

"How does the link occur? How do we implement it?" Her voice was husky, indicating her increased desire.

"All you have to do is open up your mind to mine, let me into your thoughts." He hoped she was truly sure of what she was about to do.

Yes, I am sure, Darius.

He heard the husky mind voice and knew immediately it was Leah. He felt joy until, a brief moment later, worry intruded concerning the thoughts he had been having earlier. She might not appreciate the things he wanted to do to and with her later. "How? When did you manage to link with me? You had trouble trying yesterday. I thought I would have to guide you."

"I managed it when we were returning from the shuttle. I finally realised you had different brain patterns than I was used to. It was a simple matter of altering my range. You should be pleased instead of apprehensive about my reading your thoughts. You just confirmed what I read of your memories."

Darius stood up and drew Leah to him, loving the way her body fit against his. Her head reached only to his chest, making him feel so protective of her.

She tilted her head back and looked up at him. "Why did you not tell me you were coming to care for me? I thought you were just sexually attracted to me. Why hide your feelings?"

"It is like a programming in our genes to instinctively love and care about our life mates." He thought for a moment, considering his words. "I know I am not explaining myself clearly, forgive me. It is hard to put my feelings into words. I can show you what I mean if you will let the mate link fall into place."

He watched Leah's face. Would she mate link with him? Or reject him?

"No," Leah said.

Darius's stomach churned with her words. She was rejecting him! The pain in his head grew stronger and there was a prickling behind his eyes. He had to get away from her before he took the choice out of her hands and did something he would forever regret.

Turning away from her was the hardest decision he had made in his life. If she would not come to him he would not force her. But he could not bear to be in the same room as her and know she was condemning him to a life without hope. A life without love.

"Darius, where are you going? Why do you feel so... hurt?"

He stopped walking toward the door but he answered her without turning.

"You have refused to join with me. So that I am not tempted to break my word and just take you, I am leaving." He hated the catch in his voice that would let her know the pain he felt at her decision, but he could not prevent it from coming through.

"No, Darius! I didn't mean *no*, I would not link with you. I mean *no*, I will not reject you."

He spun around. There was total sincerity in her expression. He closed the gap that separated them and pulled her into his arms.

Leah couldn't believe the pain and hurt that she'd felt pouring from Darius when he turned from her and headed for the door. Now, being in his arms caught in an unbreakable hold made her realise how strongly he cared for her. "Oh, Darius, after what I just felt coming from you, I have no doubts in my mind that everything you have said to me is the truth. I am so sorry I hurt you. I wasn't just listening to what you said but also to what you thought. It was your thoughts I was answering." Tears drenched her eyes at the desolation and pain he'd exuded just minutes ago.

They hadn't known each other long enough to fall in love yet. But if all the caring she felt from Darius was any indication, love would follow soon. She had never been in a situation like this before. Her people did not show their personal feelings to others outside of family. Even then, although she knew her parents cared for her, they never said it out loud once she had reached adult status. Even as a child the words were not said often.

The emotional displays of the Catari were going to be hard to get used to. She only hoped that it was something she would have time to learn. Her people would not simply let Ashley and her stay missing. They were probably looking for them both right now, in fact. She was then struck by the realisation that she really didn't want to be found.

For someone brought up in a self-contained society, that was something hard to admit. But even though she had known Darius and his people only for a short time, she revelled in the emotions they displayed. It was wonderful the ways her body tightened when Darius was near, and especially the way she reacted to his personal scent. Most of all she liked the way she felt protected by him.

Feeling his tight grip loosen, she tilted her head back to look up at him. All she had time to notice was his eyes before he covered her mouth with his. With a burst of freedom, she accepted his marauding tongue as he thrust it into her mouth. Duelling with his tongue and tasting his essence made opening her mind to his touch so easy.

She was aware of him as he entered a part of her mind that had never had any outside presence in it before. He laid down what looked like silken strands in that little corner of her mind. Strands that she followed to their end, secured in a part of Darius's mind that she'd missed during her previous explorations.

She watched as the strands grew and multiplied, then glowed in a shimmering silver. When that happened, her body began to tingle, starting with little fingers of movement in her mind that extended down her face and gradually over her body. Her heart gave a little lurch as though it was looking for something to attach itself to.

She felt Darius! That was the only way to describe it. She was aware of what he was thinking, of his body's reaction to holding and kissing her. Never before had she felt so special, so cared for. But from linking with Darius she knew how he saw her, how much he needed her in his life.

Breaking away from his mouth was hard, but she wanted to look at him, to try to take in these thoughts not her own. Opening her eyes she realised that the massive pain he had been feeling was reducing as the link he had placed between them took over. She was thankful for that.

Darius lowered his sweat-dampened forehead to hers and sighed. She was glad she let him mind link with her. Never again would she doubt what he told her. "Thank you, Leah. I know this has been hard for you to both accept and want. But thank you for taking a chance with me."

She felt his gratitude through their link, and knew she had done the right thing. But she also could tell that, although he didn't want to rush, things had to be completed soon. He had responsibilities that needed his personal touch, the Jageri males for one. As for herself, she needed the women's help in being prepared for the ceremony.

Jageri, so that was who they were.

Yes, they are from the Jageri people. Jarod is the alpha of his pack, and his brother Jerun is their Shaman. Both claim Ashley as their mate. Darius sounded apprehensive. Was he worried about what she would think?

Do the same rules apply to them as to you, Darius? They will love and care for her? Leah wanted to know her friend would be happy in her new life. If her experience was anything to go on, Ashley would not be able to do anything other than accept them as mates, but would Ashley accept her fate?

That was something that Leah was not completely sure of. Ashley had never been rebellious over the choice of her mate, not like herself.

Yes, little one. All Catarian can do nothing else but make their mates happy. Have no fear of that.

"As much as I want to stay here with you and answer the questions I can feel you want to ask, we both have things to do before the ceremony. I will take you to Mata and the other women who are waiting to help to prepare you for the ceremony," Darius said, stepping back.

Leah watched him. There was something else he wanted to say or ask of her but was unsure how she would react to it. He swallowed and coughed to clear his throat.

"You realise that after our Shaman joins us in the ceremony, we will join our bodies together before our people? That we will make love in front of them?" he said in a rush.

Of course! Mata had explained that to her the previous night, but she was so certain the mating ceremony would not take place, she had not listened. Now she wished she had. Would they really have to mate in public?

"I... Mata tried to explain some of the ceremony to me last night, but I didn't really listen to that part of it." Leah's face flushed scarlet from embarrassment at the thought of all his people watching her naked. "I don't know if I could cope with that. All your people seeing me with nothing on! I am sorry but I don't think I could do that even for you." She turned her face away from him.

Gentle fingers on her chin turned her face back toward him. "Do you trust me to keep you from harm? To not hurt you in any way? My people take nudity as part of our daily lives. We see nothing wrong in mates showing their affections toward each other in public. I know it is not part of your culture, but it is going to be part of your life from now on. Embrace the freedom that being my mate will bring you. Trust me to let nothing harm you."

Leah knew what he was saying made sense. *To him*! He was obviously used to running around naked and seeing naked people. But she wasn't. Could she provide what he wanted and needed from her? She supposed she could blank out everything but him. His delicious smell. How he felt when he touched her. Would that be enough of a distraction? Would she be able to forget his people were watching him love her? She would have to think about this.

"There is no time to think, little one. The ceremony is soon and I need you to trust me further. Can you do that? For me?" Darius looked into her eyes as though he was trying to tell her all would be well.

"I can try, Darius, but --"

"Do not worry. Everything will fall into place, you will see. Now let me take you to Mata and the others. They have been waiting on you for a while. You must have something to eat and drink, but relaxing in the bathing room first will make you feel better." Darius turned her around and led her toward the door.

Chapter Nine

Leah watched Darius leave. When she turned toward Mata she noticed another woman standing beside her.

"It's good to see you again, Leah. This is Jilla, the Seer of the Jageri clan. She came with her pack leader, Jarod, as well as Ashley's other mate, Jeran, to escort Ashley back to their lands."

Jilla was stunning to look at. Like the Jageri men she had dark blonde hair with streaks of gold running through it. Her eyes were the colour of topaz and her bearing was that of someone who knew her own worth. Someone happy with who she was. She dressed the same way as Mata and the other females, in the thigh-length tunic that showed off her long, tanned legs. Leah felt like a midget beside them, especially since the tunic she had been given fell below her knees.

"Leah, I want to say thank you for agreeing to join with Darius today. I know you must have had a shock after what happened at your shuttle this morning." Mata patted her hand as she said this. Leah felt warmth coming from the other woman that hadn't been there before.

"It was a shock to see Darius and the others change from cats into men. He explained some things to me, about why it was so important for us to link mind to mind. But please tell me more about your people. Everything is so overwhelming to me."

"We are of the Pantheri pack of the Leopai people. When we shift we are black in colour as you saw earlier. The various cousin lines change into a cat unique to their pack.

Some are similar in colour to the Jageri, but have different patterns on their coats. You will see some of them later today. As I said yesterday, Darius is the leader of the cousin lines and most of the alpha males will manage to attend even though the ceremony is of short notice. A mating is a time of rejoicing among our people." Mata opened the door to the bathing room as she finished.

Leah walked into the bathing room slowly, knowing there was more she would like to find out about the shape-shifting abilities of the Catari, but now didn't seem to be the time for further answers. Some of the women she had seen last night serving in the dining room were bathing already. They waved in welcome to the three new arrivals, and one left the warm water and came to meet them.

"We have everything ready for you, Mata." Smiling at Leah as she spoke, she put her hand on Leah's arm. "Please come with me and I will help you undress." She led Leah to one of the benches along the wall.

"We will use some exfoliation cream that has just been prepared, to make your skin as smooth as possible," Mata explained as she came to stand in front of Leah. "We also like to use a depilatory mixture that removes any unwanted body hair."

"Where do you… oh, you mean my pussy hair. I don't know, Mata, it seems kind of…"

"No. It need not be an extreme removal; we have two types of cream, one that will remove all hair growth permanently and another one that just removes the hairs for a few days. That is the one that we have prepared for you now. But I can assure you from personal experience that you will enjoy the sensation of having no hair growth at all."

"I… all right, let's do that, Mata, before I change my mind. I have had a similar process to this done on my other body hair before."

"Lie down now and let me apply some of this cream to your pussy. Open your legs slightly."

Leah felt herself growing steadily calmer as she drifted through her memories of her last conversation with Darius. Moving her legs apart she felt the coolness of the cream being applied to her labia and down to her anus. It gave a tingling feeling that was quite pleasant; Mata's touch was gentle as she covered her pubic hairs with cream. Leah didn't know if it was Mata's touch or her thoughts of Darius that made her pussy grow moist. This was a totally new experience for her. She couldn't wait to see Darius's reaction to her bare pussy.

"There, that is finished, now we will leave it for a little while before I remove the cream."

Leah watched as one of the other women gave a small wooden scraper and dish to Mata. When she started to remove the cream on her pussy, Leah saw her breathe in deeply. Saw the glow that came to her eyes before she quickly closed them.

"Mata, are you okay?"

"Yes, I am fine. Let me finish this quickly."

Leah noticed the extra care she gave as she removed her hair, how fingers seemed to linger near her clit. But she never felt threatened, never thought that Mata would do something she never wanted her to do. All too soon the cream was removed and Mata handed the scraper to one of her helpers.

She was quite sorry it finished so quickly. She wanted to explore these strange feelings… well, unfamiliar to her anyway. The two of the females in the pool were on really friendly terms. Stroking and washing each other, touching each other in such a way that Leah knew they were lovers.

"Stand up, Leah, and we will use the exfoliation cream next."

Leah stood motionless as Jilla helped Mata rub the granulated cream using a circular movement until her body was completely covered in the lavender scented cream. The experience of having two women massage the grains onto her sensitive skin made her tingle all over in reaction to their touch. Her nipples were taut buds, and her skin felt too tight for her frame. Leah noticed that she was not the only one who looked aroused. Both Mata and Jilla were visibly stimulated by the looks of them.

"Now you need to step into the pool and wash off all the grains."

She stepped into the pool and sat on the ledge. Two other women washed her body clear of the grains. It was nice being pampered this way, and she closed her eyes to better enjoy it. A quick duck under the water wet her hair, and within seconds she experienced a soothing massage on her scalp and the sweet scent of lavender cleanser. She sighed with pleasure.

Leah allowed Mata and Jilla to rub a lavender-fragranced lotion over her back, arms and legs before they completed their own toilets. One of the other women helped Leah into a lovely pale lilac tunic.

"This fits me," said Leah in surprise when she noticed that the tunic was thigh-length like the rest of the women's clothes.

"We had it made for you once we knew that the ceremony would take place today. More are being prepared for you." Mata guided Leah toward the door. "Come, let us go to the dining room and we will have something to eat and drink. You will be ready for the ceremony after that."

Chapter Ten

Standing with Kell and waiting for the arrival of Leah was a harrowing experience for Darius; he knew she was still apprehensive about the mating part of the ceremony.

Having to deal with the Jageri was something he would have preferred not to do, but they had to realise they couldn't run wild on his territory. They were not happy with his decision to place two men as guards on each of them, but this was *his* territory. He set the rules.

Kell nudged him to get his attention. Darius followed Kell's gaze to where Leah and the rest of the women were leaving the stronghold and moving into the courtyard where his people were gathered for the ceremony.

His breath caught in his throat at the lovely picture Leah made in one of the traditional tunics of the Leopai women. The women had made it to his colour specifications especially for her, and it pleased him to see her in clothes that accentuated her beautiful body. He knew the exact moment she became aware of him. Her eyes opened wide at the sight of him in his traditional mating ceremony covering; she stood still for a minute just looking at him.

He saw the calm look she gave Mata before she began the walk toward him, the confident glance she cast to his people who were eagerly watching her every move. He was so proud of the way she had reacted to everything that had been thrown at her since arriving on his world. A lesser woman would have crumbled at the expectations put on such delicate shoulders.

Taking Leah's hand in his as she reached him, he leaned down and brushed a quick kiss over her flushed and rosy cheek. From the corner of his eye he saw the Shaman approach.

"Darius, introduce me to your mate. I am sorry we haven't had a chance to talk before this."

"Leah, this is our Shaman, Aaron. He will join us as mates today." Darius gave her arm a squeeze, trying to make her realise without words how important the Shaman was to the Leopai.

"I am delighted you are finally here, Leah."

"Thank you, it is nice to meet you too," said Leah, before giving Darius a quick glance.

"Come, it is time for the joining." The Shaman led Leah by the arm as Darius moved to her other side. And they walked to the altar in front of the crowd.

"Darius and Leah are here to be joined as one," Aaron announced to the assembled Leopai.

Aaron turned to face both of them. "Darius, take Leah's right hand in yours." The Shaman picked up a length of cording from the altar and bound their hands together. He turned back toward the altar, lifted the ceremonial stole and placed it over his shoulders, then lifted a jewelled dagger. "Darius, will you say the joining words to Leah?"

Darius looked into Leah's eyes. "I claim you as my mate. I will protect and care for you, cherish and love you until the day I die. I take you as my mate, never to be separate again."

As he said the words of joining, Darius felt a pull on his heart as he waited for the words to be said in return.

While Darius made his vows Leah was drawn to him. In a whole new way. There was a sense of peace, of belonging. Of being whole. Yet there was also tension. Relief would come in only one way. She *had* to say the words back to him. In that moment, anything else was impossible. Somehow she knew what to say, though where the words came from she didn't know.

"I accept you as my mate. I will love and care for you, cherish and stand by your side till the day I die. I take you as my mate, never to be separate again." As she said the words, the tension that had built snapped, the pressure eased, and she found herself joined even deeper with Darius than she had been before.

Aaron cut the cord from their wrists, then took Darius's hand and made a shallow cut on his palm. As he turned to her, she remembered what Mata had told her about the mingling of blood in the ceremony. He took her hand and made a shallow cut on her palm. Gentle though he was, her palm stung like fire!

She watched as Aaron brought their cut palms together and tied them with another cord.

"The joining words have been spoken. The mingling of blood is complete. All that remains is the physical joining of your bodies."

Leah jumped as a cheer burst from the waiting people, and Darius turned her toward the crowd, as though presenting her. She had forgotten they were there, since all of her attention was taken up with Darius and the emotions running back and forth from the link that had grown stronger with their simple words.

"What did the mingling of blood do?" she quietly asked her mate. Yes, she could admit that's what he was, now. In truth, she had recognised him from the first time they met.

"It helps to complete the joining; it will help with the transformation you will go through." His answer was equally quiet.

"Transformation? What transformation?" Leah gasped out.

"You will become like me, Leah, a Pantheri of the Leopai people."

A shiver ran through Leah when she heard *that* news. She would become like him? Be able to transform into an animal? When would that happen?

Warming all over at the image Darius projected into her mind, Leah's pussy grew wet. She wanted that image to become reality. Now! Even with all his people watching. Somehow, with the mingling of his blood, she apparently was losing her inhibitions.

Aaron untied the cord from their wrists, and placed his own palms over their cuts. A tingling heat ran through her hand and up her arm, spreading until it covered her breasts and made her nipples harden into tight kernels that strained through the tunic she had on.

Darius gave a low growl at the sight of them. Looking into his eyes, eyes clouded with desire for her, she lifted her face, straining to join his lips with hers.

Aaron moved away from the two of them as Darius took her shoulders and pulled her to his body. The warmth of his lips met hers, and she opened her mouth to him. His tongue tangled with hers as they explored each other with a passion never felt before. It was the amazingly rough but gentle tongue of his that enhanced her sensations. His hand touched one nipple, rolling the hard point between two fingers, pulling on it slightly, just enough to make her pussy flood with moisture.

He unfastened the ties at the shoulders of her tunic. The air hit her now bare skin, from shoulders to breast. He lowered his head to her exposed breast and sucked on her nipple, gently at first, then with stronger suction until she heard herself moaning out loud. Her stomach tightened with all the delicious feelings he was stirring inside her.

Vaguely she was aware of movement in the gathering of his -- and now her people, but all her attention was taken up by what Darius was doing to her body. He had managed to completely move her tunic so it only covered her lower body. His hands slowly moved over her stomach and tugged the tunic over her hips until it pooled at her feet. She should have been embarrassed knowing she was totally exposed to the watching crowd, but she could only concentrate on the tingling in her nipples and the warmth of the moisture from her arousal as it trickled down her leg.

She was experiencing pleasure from both his hands and mouth, but mostly from the link she shared with him. It was strange to feel how her nipple tasted in his mouth and to experience the pull on it at the same time. The link provided double the pleasure and it was completely turning her into an exhibitionist!

Darius gently pushed her legs apart. Leah was all for that happening, so she moved to allow him access to the centre of her body. As his fingers parted her labial folds and gently stroked her clit, she heard herself moan as he moved from her breast. His eyes glowed from his normal deep blue to a silvery glow and back as he discovered for himself that she now had a hair-free pussy. He ran his fingers carefully over her bare mound.

"Touch me, Leah! I need the touch of your hands on me," Darius moaned, and then returned his attention to her nipples.

Leah tugged at the ties on the very brief loincloth Darius had worn to the ceremony. It was even briefer than the ones he normally wore and was a darker colour than her gown. She managed to loosen it enough to slide her hands under the waistband and stroke his stomach muscles. His *hard* stomach muscles. She moved her hands further down. Down toward his straining cock.

One finger running over the length of his cock provoked a purr against her nipple, a reaction that let her know he liked her touch. She grew bolder in her exploration and pushed the covering over his hips, letting it fall to the ground.

His cock was far too thick for her to close her hand over it completely, but she gently took as much as she could in one hand and ran a finger over the tip. A bead of moisture formed, and she wiped it with her finger. Darius lifted his head. She brought her finger to her mouth slowly, and his eyes followed her movements with hunger. She sucked the pre-come from her finger, licking it and enjoying his musky taste. He groaned then buried his head at her breast, purring heavily. He nipped her nipple lightly with his teeth, and she groaned in response.

Leah pulled away from him, not in pain but because she wanted to actually *see* what she held in her hand. She took in every detail; the thick, long length of him, the ruddy tip that was again leaking pre-ejaculate and the way the shaft twitched as she studied him with interest.

But study him was not all she wanted to do. Looking up, she took in the way his upper lip was covered in a light sheen of sweat, and the way his eyes still flickered between deep blue and the glow of passion for her. He placed his hands on her shoulders and gently pushed her to her knees in front of his straining erection.

It was easy to understand what he wanted her to do, and as it agreed with her own wishes, she caressed him with her hand, slowly and deliberately. Back and forth, up and down, her hand stroked his cock. Moving her mouth nearer the leaking tip, she touched him with her tongue and licked away the drop of liquid sitting there. This small taste of him was not enough, so she opened her mouth to take the tip of his cock in as far as she could. Over and over she ran her tongue around the outside edge and back toward the small hole on the end.

She knew he enjoyed the sensation of her mouth on his cock, both from the mate link and from the way his breath caught in his throat. At the same time she sucked and licked, her hand stroked all of him she couldn't fit into her mouth. The amount of pre-come increased with her actions, and she eagerly lapped it from him. Darius held her head as she moved in a rhythm with her strokes.

"Enough!" he growled. "I don't want to come in your mouth this first time." He pulled away from her mouth and dragged her body up until she stood tight against his own, then he covered her mouth with his.

Breaking away from the passionate kiss that left her dazed, Leah watched as Darius dropped down on his knees and latched onto her clit with his mouth. The little nibbles he made with his teeth caused her to open her legs wider so he could more easily have access to the heart of her body. The shivers that ran through her body when he touched her and the way his tongue made its way into the depths of her naked pussy stimulated her body to release more of its liquid into his waiting mouth.

Leah knew her orgasm was near -- his tongue had that effect on her body. She loved the rough texture of it, knew she would never get enough of it.

"Darius, I am going to come soon," she told him in a breathless voice. He lifted his face to look up at her, his mouth and chin covered in moisture from her pussy juices. With a seductive glint in his eyes, he licked his lips clean.

Standing up, he gave her another kiss, letting her taste and smell her own musky feminine aroma, then turned her so that her back was against his chest. This forced her to face the crowd witnessing his claiming of her. She had forgotten them up until this point; Darius had made sure of that by keeping her occupied with thoughts of him.

But now, seeing them watch with rapt attention made her feel self-conscious all over again.

Darius must have felt her hesitation because he bent his head to whisper in her ear. "Don't pay any attention to them. Concentrate on what I am doing, on the pleasure that my loving gives to you." He cupped her breasts in his large hands, squeezing her nipples until she closed her eyes, moaning at the tingles running through her.

Leah shivered from the wild sensations running down her spine as Darius placed small kisses from her ear down the side of her neck. Stopping where her shoulder met her neck, he took little nibbling bites, and then sucked on the skin of that sensitive area.

Darius pushed on her shoulders gently, urging her to her knees. She felt him as he knelt behind her, his hands still on her shoulders. He bent his head to whisper in her ear once more. "Lean forward, little one. Put your hands on the ground and let me see your pussy and ass from a different angle."

Leah flushed all over. His words made her pussy throb in pleasure. His breath was hot on her buttocks as he brought his face nearer the rosette of her anus. Never had she expected to feel the swipe of his tongue there, but he licked her once, then twice.

"Open your legs for me."

She obeyed his command and moved her legs apart as far as was comfortable. The length of his tongue stroked over her pussy from her clit to the opening of her anus and back. His purring become louder, and a growl sounded from deep in his throat.

He moved back from his ministrations and she looked over her shoulder at him. As he stared at her his eyes glowed, rapidly flickering from one colour to the other. He took his shaft in hand and moved closer to her, finally touching the entrance to her pussy with the tip of his cock. *Skyla*! She closed her eyes at the overwhelming sensations swirling through her body; the tightening and the contractions started deep in her pussy.

"Are you ready for my claiming? Are you as needy as I am at this moment? Does the fact that my people are watching our every move still embarrass you?" Darius said huskily, demanding an answer.

Leah moved her hips backwards in wordless response, telling him in a more direct way than with speech that she wanted him to take her. Now!

"Ah, I can see that you want me as much as I want you, my love."

With that, she felt the surge that he gave his hips, and the thick, long length of his cock worked its way into the hidden depths of her pussy. His thickness made him go slower than she wanted, but she was grateful he was so careful of her comfort. He moved back slightly then pushed in again, going further than before. Soon, he was balls deep in her pussy.

He was so long she felt the tip of his cock touch the entrance of her womb. She had never before been so full, and she loved it. Giving her hips a little push backwards, she heard Darius groan. He gripped her hips in his strong hands and started the timeless in and out motion.

He was going too slowly for her; she wanted him to fuck her faster and harder!

"Faster, Darius! Please go faster. I can feel myself about to come," she gasped to her mate.

"You want it faster? Then you shall get your wish." Darius groaned as he increased the speed of his movement. He thrust his hips forward and backward as hard as he could. It was still not enough for her.

Leah felt Darius move his hand around to touch her clit, pinching it in time with his thrusts. She felt the pleasure of his penetration deep in the depths of her pussy.

Darius must have been aware of this as his movements became even harder and he nibbled at her neck again. Lapping his tongue over her pulse point on her neck produced tingles that ran all over her body. But when he scraped his teeth over her shoulder and broke the skin, blinding pain shot through her. Then molten lava raced through her veins as she felt the suction of his mouth on the wound he had made on her neck.

The pleasure-pain was enough to send her over the edge into her orgasm. As her body tightened and contracted around his cock, she felt hot spurts in her pussy as Darius found his own release.

Leah felt him break away from her neck, then the lap of his tongue over the marks his teeth made. She knew she should complain about his treatment, but she was so linked in thought with him that she understood why he did this…

It was a strange sensation, to know without words why he had done it. Why he was carefully licking the wound now. Why she was letting him put his mark on her. And why she was having all these weird sensations throughout her body.

Darius had to force himself to stop taking any more of her rich, delicious blood. That could wait until she was fully transformed. Thankfully Leah had been linked closely with him throughout the claiming and was aware of the significance of his bite.

The blood exchange at the beginning of the ceremony had started the work of transforming her body's chemistry in preparation for her change. The enzymes in his saliva and his semen would work to complete that change.

The bite? Well, that was for himself. He wanted everyone to know she was his mate!

"Are you all right, my love? I didn't hurt you too much?" he asked in between licks on her neck. He could never get enough of her taste. His senses were so acute that even this early he could taste the changes that were taking place in her body.

Reluctantly he pulled out of the snug warmth of her pussy. Oh, how he wished he could stay there. But he could tell she was again growing uneasy at being so much on display. He was proud of the way she had hidden her embarrassment from his people. She would make a fine alpha female for his pack and the Leopai cousin lines. No one of Catari birth could have made a better mate for him.

He heard Leah draw in her breath as his cock slipped free from her pussy. Catching her thoughts, he knew she was slightly sore. No wonder, after the pummelling he had given her when they were caught up in their passion for each other.

"Stay like that for a minute, little one. I will clean you of my seed. My saliva has a healing agent in it and you will not be in discomfort for long." He bent his head and cleaned Leah of the combined juices of their release. He took special care at the entrance to her beautiful pussy, making sure he cleansed as far as he could reach with his tongue. Licking down over her moist folds, to her anal rosette and back, he let his healing saliva soothe her soreness. He loved her bare pussy; he knew he had Mata to thank for this treat. Through the mate link, he knew she was reluctant to let him clean her this way, but this was part of the mating. A Catari male washed his mate after claiming; it was only right to see that your mate was not left in any discomfort from your passion.

Finishing his pleasant task, a task that had his mate moaning out loud, he stood up and helped Leah to her feet to stand beside him. Looking out over his people he saw that they were caught up in their own pleasure, each finding their mates, or if unmated, willing participants to join them. There were groups of three or four enjoying each other's attentions. One particular group held Kell, Mata and Andre, his other beta. Mata was on her knees and had Kell's cock in her pussy, while sucking Andre's cock deep into her mouth. Darius knew the celebrations would go on into the night.

He picked up Leah's gown. "Let me help you with your gown, my love. You will feel better when you are covered." He lifted it over her head and smoothed it over her body. Then he covered himself, knowing Leah would feel more at ease now that they were once again clothed.

"Come, there is food waiting for us over by the tables." He held out his arm, showing the display of refreshments they had available. "Would you like something to eat or drink?"

"Just a drink. I am so thirsty."

He filled two goblets and returned to his mate, setting them on the table next to her. Gently he lifted her in his arms, cuddling her body close to his own as he sat and reached for a goblet. "Are you feeling well?"

"I am fine, apart from a... a sensation like lots of butterflies in my stomach. What is causing that?"

"It is your body changing and adapting itself to the new life you will lead with me. It will take a few days for your body to completely change. You should not feel pain, just mild discomfort."

"When you finish your drink, my love, we will leave for our own chambers. There are things I still want to do with you that I haven't been able to yet." He projected the image in her mind of him fucking her tight ass from behind. Watching her reaction, and seeing the rosy glow on her beautiful face, he knew she anticipated his possession as much as he did.

"Darius, my people will not just let Ashley and I disappear. They will be searching for us. I am afraid for your... *our* people when they find us here." Leah turned away from watching the celebrating crowd and buried her face in his chest. Darius heard the deep inhalation she took as she drew his scent into her lungs. He was glad that his presence affected her in the same way that she affected him.

"Have no fears, little one. We are not the primitive culture that you think us to be. We live as we do out of choice. Believe me when I say that you and Ashley will not be forced back with the people of your birth. I say that because you now belong to the people of Catari. You are a Leopai female and will be protected as such."

Watching as Leah lifted her face up to him, Darius took in the sight of her features. The beautiful shiny blonde hair, the stubborn look to her chin, her sensual mouth and her lovely green eyes -- eyes that were no longer clouded by anger as on their first meeting, but filled by the warmth that she was beginning to feel for him.

"I belong here now, Darius. Even if I wanted to return to my life with my people I would not, could not leave you. Not now!" She turned her head back to face the group of their people, watching as some broke away from their pleasures and made their way to the waiting tables for nourishment.

"Yes, my love, you belong here with me. Now let us go to our room, and leave our people to celebrate our joining. Put away unhappy thoughts to another day. Let us celebrate our new beginnings, together."

Epilogue

Leah breathed in the clean forest scent. The continual sensation of butterflies in her stomach had faded this morning. Darius knew the instant that happened and dragged her out of the stronghold without a word.

He had acted as tour guide the last few days, wanting her to know the area around the compound. But this place… he hadn't shown her this beautiful area before. The forest soothed her mind and body. The different shades of green of the trees and plants complemented the flowers of reds and orange that grew in and around them… and in the middle was a beautiful pool.

"I wanted to wait till the change was complete; this is a perfect spot for you to practice shifting for the first time," said Darius as he pulled her against him. "Relax, look into my mind and take the picture of my Leopai form as a guide."

Leah calmed herself and did as he said, following his thoughts as though she had been doing this for years. It never failed to surprise her how she had accepted their mate link so quickly -- so easily. Especially when she remembered how silly she had behaved when she discovered that Darius had accessed her memories of…

"Leah! Concentrate!" Darius growled.

She followed his thought pattern, seeing his animal form take shape. Leah was aware when he released his hold on her hips and moved in front of her. Opening her eyes, she watched as he became the animal so clearly revealed in his thoughts.

Follow my lead, hold the feminine version in your mind. Let the change take shape. I will hold it for you the first time.

Leah found it surprisingly easy to follow his instructions. Her bones started popping and altering shape. Her hands changed to paws before her eyes. She found herself on all fours, as the change continued seemingly all by itself. Leah was amazed that all she felt was mild discomfort. She had wondered if reshaping herself this way would hurt. But it didn't.

She found she could smell animals that hid in the forest around them; she hadn't known they were even there as they didn't make any noise. But she knew where each of them hid from the two large cats that had invaded their sanctuary.

This is amazing, Darius. It is all so vivid, so different. Leah became aware of another scent growing more intense every minute. The large cat that was Darius rubbed his head against her neck, and purred in her ear.

Instinct took over, and Leah bounded away from him, snarling a challenge to catch her if he could. She caught a laugh in his mind before she closed off contact with the big male who wanted to claim her… and ran.

Leaping over downed trees and bush, Leah was aware in the back of her mind that Darius let her have this freedom; he wanted her to run and find joy in her new shape. As that thought took over, she came back fully to her normal human thinking… and slowed her strides.

Darius… what happened?

You were taken over by animal instinct, little one. It was natural. Come, let us return to our pool.

Leah stopped and turned, waiting for his guidance and touch, then both ran in the direction of the pool, side by side.

Darius stopped her with his body, rubbing himself over her coat. His scent was even stronger than before. It was having an effect on her new shape. She turned her head into his shoulder and caught his skin between her teeth, stopping all movement from him.

He tasted delicious, she thought as she let him go.

Darius moved again, further down her body, and without hesitation buried his face in her feminine centre. She had been wet before with excitement at the chase, but now she flooded his mouth with her juices. The rasping of his tongue stung, but the pleasure-pain was so good.

Leah wiggled her hips at him, wanting something more than just his tongue, no matter how wonderful it made her feel. She wanted his cock in her body, wanted to join with him in this shape.

She felt him withdraw his tongue and turned her head, snarling a demand at him to get a move on. She caught a look at the size of his cock jutting out between his hind legs.

No way is that thing going to fit.

It will. Your body has changed to accommodate my size in this shape. We will fit together as before.

She caught the laughter in his voice at her concern. But she lost her train of thought when he entered her with a careful thrust that she felt right to her centre.

So full, so good, she thought as he stopped and waited till she adjusted to his size then started moving in and out of her pussy. He covered her body so completely with his larger size. She felt him grasp the skin at the side of her neck in his large teeth and hold her down in position for his thrusts.

The pleasure of his fast movements brought her to climax so fast that she was surprised at the roar she gave as her pussy contracted about his cock, pushing him over the edge into his own bellow of satisfaction.

Leah collapsed on the ground, taking Darius with her. He licked the skin at the side of her neck and moved his cock in and out of her body in slow movements till she became aware of her surroundings again. She heard his thoughts of contentment, and answered them with her own. How lucky she was to have found a love as strong as his.

Catari Heat 2: Double the Pleasure

Kyla Logan

Prologue

Jeran moved his cock in and out of the hot, wet mouth of the female Jageri; he enjoyed the warm swipe of her tongue as she caressed the leaking tip.

He glanced over the girl's back to his twin brother. Jarod fucked her pussy from behind in time to her moans of pleasure. Looking at his brother was like looking into a mirror. Both had golden streaks running through their hair from exposure to the sun, and eyes that changed from amber to golden depending on their mood. They were tall, muscular men, identical in every way, apart from the scar on Jarod's face, and the fact that he was the Alpha male of the Jageri people of Catari.

Jeran froze as a feeling of fear overwhelmed him. It was not coming from his brother, the only one he was mind linked intimately with. Bringing his eyes back to focus on Jarod, he saw that his brother had stopped fucking the girl too, much to her annoyance.

"What was that?" Jarod asked.

"I have no idea." Jeran's attention was focused on locating the female who was in fear for her life. The call they'd both heard was undoubtedly feminine in origin.

Jeran's cock grew soft as he pulled himself from the mouth of the girl they had been fucking. He only half listened as his brother told the girl to leave. The girl threw them a disappointed look as she left.

Jeran turned and walked over to the window and leaned on the ledge. Closing his eyes, he entered his Shaman vision quest trance. He sensed Jarod moving nearer, the other man knowing his presence would not disturb Jeran's task.

Following the unusual path of the call was difficult. He had never felt a mind pattern like this before. She was obviously *not* of Catari. And if she was not of Catari, she could only be their long awaited mate.

A mate who was in fear for her life!

Our mate? Are you sure, my brother? Jarod asked.

Jeran opened himself further and let his brother follow where he travelled, in search of their mate. What they saw made their hearts stop.

Their mate was in a spacecraft, crashing onto their world. She was attempting to fasten herself into a seat, but was unable to close and secure the straps that would hold her safe. Jeran and Jarod winced in sympathy as they felt the bones in one of her arms snap when the craft crashed into a forest. Then, with a sharp pain they felt in their heads, the link was abruptly severed.

She'd lost consciousness.

"Which direction?" asked Jarod, in an understandably agitated voice.

"It crashed on the hunting grounds of the Pantheri," Jeran replied, aware of Jarod's growing displeasure at his answer. The Leopai, in particular the Pantheri pack, had been the Jageri's enemies. Now after the call for solidarity with the various packs of Catari, it was a reluctant peace that they had with each other.

Going to their former enemy's lands to claim their mate was not something either of them wanted to do. Especially Jarod! His scar, the result of a *friendly* scuffle at a joint pack gathering only two seasons ago, was testament to the unwilling truce they had with the Pantheri Alpha, Darius.

Chapter One

All Jeran saw of Jarod's expression before teleporting out of his sight was the frown on his face. But Jeran had heard a cry from his mate. Someone, or something, had disturbed her enough that she'd reached out to him again. It worried him, this coma she had been in these past four days. Only he had heard her cry, as Jarod was not as powerful with mind touch as he was.

He'd gasped out to his twin brother and Alpha that their mate was calling to him. Then he did something he'd been reluctant to expose to the other packs before, the Pantheri in particular. He shimmered and teleported himself into his mate's room. While rematerializing he became aware she was not alone. Her friend from the crash and now Alpha female of the Pantheri sat on the pallet beside her. Masking his arrival by keeping his body out of phase with normal time, he listened to what she was saying, hoping to gain insight as to what had triggered his mate's cry for help.

"Oh, Ash, you would never believe what has happened since we arrived on this planet. If I'd known what to expect when we left our base ship to explore, I would do it all again. The only thing I would change is your lying here injured."

Jeran looked down at the two of them, wondering if he'd imagined the flicker of Ashley's eyelashes as Leah talked to her.

It pained him to see his mate lying so still. She was so beautiful with shoulder-length ash blonde hair and a full mouth with pouting lips. He didn't know what colour eyes she had, but he looked forward with great anticipation to her opening them so he could see. Like her friend, she was of petite build. She'd be lucky if she came up to his breastbone when standing next to him. She made him feel protective of her. That was the only word to describe it. Her fragile beauty brought out the animal in him. No one would hurt her again. Why had no one warned him of this built-in compulsion to protect his mate at all costs?

"I have a mate now, a wonderful man. Well, not just a man, as you will see when you wake. I am not the same person I was before either. This morning for the first time, I discovered what it is like to run like a cat. It is amazing, feeling the power in the muscles of your legs as you run. You will find that out for yourself, too, when you awaken," Leah continued.

He wondered what brought the rosy glow to her cheeks as she said that. It looked as though it was travelling all over her body. If he took the time he could find out, but he'd used a considerable amount of energy by travelling in his unorthodox way. He needed to reserve the rest for healing his mate completely.

There! That was another flicker of Ashley's lashes. It was time to announce his presence to her friend Leah, but how to do so and not give away his secret quite yet?

Returning to the doorway, he projected an image of the door opening and himself entering the room into Leah's mind.

She looked startled by his arrival. No wonder! Darius had made sure only Jilla, the Jageri Seer, out of all the Jageri, was allowed near her.

Leah watched him intently as he moved further into the room and approached the opposite side of Ashley's pallet. He could feel her eyes on him as he stared down at his injured mate.

"She has not moved at all since you arrived?" he asked her.

Leah cleared her throat before answering him.

"Unfortunately not. Can you tell me what you are called?" she asked him. "No one has seen fit to introduce us."

Jeran gave a small grin as she asked this. He was certain her mate was rushing to her side following her surprise at his arrival in the room.

"I am Jeran. My brother is called Jarod. I'm surprised Darius has let you out of his sight. My brother and I thought we would not meet with you again until our mate wakened," he answered, turning his attention back to Ashley.

As he spoke, the door to the room swung open, almost crashing against the wall. Darius filled the doorway, breath heaving as if he had run all the way from wherever he'd been.

Jeran watched Darius stride across the floor toward Leah and stand protectively by her side. He could tell Darius was annoyed from the way his body moved and knew the displeasure was directed at him.

"I thought I told you to stay with two of my men when you were on my territory. How did you get past them and why are you here when my mate is visiting her friend?" Darius growled out the words as he glared at Jeran.

"I didn't realise your mate was with *my* mate, Darius. And you know I will not give away Shaman secrets to you." Jeran smirked, watching Darius fight to keep his temper under control.

Darius turned toward Leah. "You will be able to visit Ashley in peace later, my mate. I have something to show you in our quarters."

Leah complied without argument. As she reached the doorway, she turned back toward the pallet where Ashley lay.

Jeran studied his mate, looking for telltale signs that she might be awakening. He felt Leah's gaze before she turned and left the room with Darius.

Chapter Two

Jeran stopped smirking the minute the door closed behind Ashley's friend and her irate mate. He knew he shouldn't have rubbed it in Darius's face that his security precautions had no meaning for a Shaman. Seeing his mate lying still and silent had him behaving out of character.

Once again he focused all his attention on the still body of his mate. He'd attempted to deep heal the injuries to her body for the last three days. Each time the treatment revived her slightly; this should be the last time he would have to use his power. It was growing difficult to focus on healing Ashley while suffering from the painful reaction of not being able to lay claim to his mate.

If the Seer and Shaman of the Leopai had assisted Jilla and himself with the healing, it would've been so much quicker. But Mata's powers were not in healing, but in foretelling, and he was reluctant to trust his mate's mind with someone he did not fully know… or trust. Also, even though Aaron was a fellow Shaman, he was still a former enemy.

He didn't have to look up to see who entered the room when the door opened. He'd been aware of his brother striding quickly through the corridors with his silent watchers and jailers behind him.

"How is she? Have you attempted further healing?" Jarod rumbled as he walked to the other side of their sleeping mate. "I thought you were waiting on Jilla to combine your powers."

"I couldn't just sit there waiting for permission to visit our mate. I apologise for disappearing and leaving you to explain to our guards. I felt her call to me; I had to come as quickly as I could."

"What caused her to reach out to you again? I'd feel jealous if I didn't know her call was weak and the distance too great for me to hear her. When you've been in a healing trance I am aware of her calls because of our link." Jarod sat on the edge of the pallet and took the limp hand of his mate in his own. "I will be glad when our mate link is in place so that I always know her thoughts."

Jarod began to feel the all encompassing pain in his head and body again due to the proximity of his unclaimed mate. He and Jeran had not rebelled too often against the orders of Darius because it was painful to be in such close contact with Ashley and not claim her by linking their minds together. To do so without her knowledge or consent were the actions of a savage; neither of them wanted to take a step backward to their forefathers' time when such a thing was the norm. She deserved the courtesy of free choice. Although, that might not be possible if she remained unconscious much longer. Jarod knew that Jeran found each healing more difficult because of the physical pain he endured because they had not completing the mate link. If he could not focus, he couldn't heal her. What was more important to them? Her life? Or their honour?

"Her life! You know there's no other choice, my Alpha. If I can't heal the remaining injuries to her head, then we must link with her totally. It's the only way. We both know that." Jeran looked up from the body of their mate to stare into Jarod's eyes.

Jarod knew Jeran was right, but it was a choice neither of them would feel happy making. Hearing the door open, Jarod looked up and saw Jilla enter the room. He wasn't pleased when Mata followed closely behind her.

"Mata will try to assist us. You know that extra power will help, Jeran. If I thought you would accept it, I would've dragged their Shaman here too!" Jilla was determined they would accept Mata's aid.

"I know I am not as powerful in healing as in other areas, but I will give you all the power at my disposal with pleasure. Ashley is the friend of my Alpha. I can do no other than help you heal her." Mata moved nearer to the sleeping pallet.

Jarod looked at Jeran, sensing his reluctance in accepting this offered help. He knew that he might have to order it if there was a chance the extra power would be the trigger in bringing their mate to consciousness.

Jeran glared first at Jarod, then Mata. "Very well, I accept your offer. But be warned, anything you see or hear you will tell no one. I want your word on that, Seer."

Jarod was thankful he didn't have to force Jeran's acceptance. The healing was stressful enough without there being any ill feeling between these two. He knew the pain in Jeran's body was making his brother behave uncharacteristically. Jarod was the more temperamental of the two, but then he'd not been using power the way Jeran had. No wonder Jeran was showing signs of fatigue. Hopefully, this healing session would be the last and then they could get to know their mate and claim her as their own.

He tried to defuse the situation. "Mata is a Seer with as much integrity as Jilla. She will not divulge any of your healing methods. Where do you want us to stand so we can link for the healing?"

"Jilla, stand beside me. Mata, go to Jarod's side," Jeran ordered.

Once everyone was in place they linked with each other's minds in the general mind meld. Jeran joined him with ease; Jilla followed just as easily, as she'd linked with them many times in the past.

Mata was a little hesitant, even though she'd offered her power. Jarod knew why she was reluctant to enter the link; Jeran did not exactly welcome her.

"Oh, for goodness sake, Mata, come on. I don't bite. Well, not much. We're thankful that you are willing to help us, please enter," Jeran muttered through clenched teeth.

Jarod was aware of Mata entering the link with them, felt her unique power flowing through. No, she was not a strong healer, but she could still focus her power on helping them heal Ashley.

Watching as his brother gathered their energy and made it his own was a joy to see. Jarod was in awe of the power his twin carried with grace. Jeran was also Alpha, and powerful enough that he could have left the pack and started his own, but their love for each other kept him by Jarod's side, always helping, but never undermining Jarod's leadership.

Now, all Jarod could do was continue feeding Jeran energy… he only hoped it would be enough.

Chapter Three

Ashley heard the voice in her mind again. It was always there, waiting for her to acknowledge its existence. She could ignore it for a time, but it always became more insistent, wanting a response. Sometimes another voice joined it in its call to her. When that happened the pain became unbearable and she tried to hide from it. She knew why it was here now though. She'd called out for help. She needed to answer Leah, to let her know she was in here -- somewhere -- and that she couldn't break free.

She seemed to have been in this barren wasteland forever, trying to find her way back to her friend's side. The sun beat down on her constantly; there was no night, just endless hot, dry heat.

At first, she couldn't move her arm, but after hearing the voice for the first time -- or was it the second -- small movement occurred. Too quickly, she was losing track of what had happened. Was it days or weeks that she had been trapped here? If she wasn't found soon, she would be lost here forever!

But now they wanted her to join them. She knew the pain it caused them when they were too close to her. She didn't want them to hurt so much, so she tried to hide from their voices. Even though she wanted out of this place, she didn't want to be the cause of their pain.

Amazingly she could see the features of the voices. At first, she'd thought they were the same, but she could now tell them apart. How beautiful they were to look upon. She knew they would not want her to call them that. They were too masculine in their attitude to want to be called something so feminine. But to her eyes they were the most beautiful beings she'd ever seen.

Tall, so tall she would feel like a child standing beside them. Hair the colour of wheat with lighter streaks running through it, and those eyes! She loved their eyes; she'd never seen eyes that changed colour like theirs did. From amber to gold they changed back and forth. To say nothing of their full and sensuous lips. Lips she would love to feel on hers.

She would hurt them if she left this place to be with them. She didn't want that to happen but they were becoming more insistent that she obey them. Now they had someone else to help them find her; she didn't recognise this voice at all. There was something familiar about it all the same.

If only Leah were here, she could try to tell her about the voices being hurt; she would know how to stop it. Ashley remembered the last time they were with her…

* * *

Ashley raised her eyes upward when she heard the sound of footsteps on the ground. She was startled to see two men standing in front of her. She could see them plainly this time. How tall they were, and how naked! Long, golden tanned limbs, wide muscled chests, and thick, stiff cocks.

"What? What are you doing here? You will be trapped if you stay with me," she said, panicking, not just because they had joined her in this horrible place, but because of the reaction of her body. They had to see the hard pointed outline of her nipples through her torn uniform.

She had never had this reaction to any man before. Certainly not with Keevan, her intended mate back home. But, these two! Just their gaze made her body react. Her pussy grew moist, and they knew it; she could see by the deep breath both took that they could smell her feminine arousal. It's a good thing this was only a dream otherwise she'd be very embarrassed.

She fully intended to take advantage of this situation. Her dreams back on her base ship had just whetted her appetite. What better way to forget how trapped she was than to play with these two figures of male perfection?

"You know us, Ashley. You called to us and here we are," said the tall figure on the right.

"How do you know my name? Who are you?" Ashley stood up and walked nearer to them. She knew they wouldn't harm her; they never had before -- before they had made her feel so much better.

"Let us pleasure you, Ashley. We want to take care of you," said the man on her left. He moved closer until he could cup her face in his large hands, bringing her mouth toward his. Ashley opened her lips to accept the thrust of his tongue against her own. Running her hands through his thick, golden hair, loving the soft, silky texture of his long locks, she was not surprised to feel the other male close to her back. He ran his hands over her shoulders and arms, drawing her uniform down her body to her waist, and then moved his hands around her naked torso, cupping her breasts in gentle hands.

Breaking free from the kiss, Ashley turned her head, hoping to find the mouth of her second lover and was pleased when he seemed to know what she needed. His kiss was as gentle as his touch, not as overpowering as the first one, but just as sensual. His hands still massaged her nipples when she felt the warm mouth of her first lover take one of the taut buds in his mouth and suck strongly on it. The pulling of his mouth, the tugging of her other nipple, and the tongue duelling with her own were too much for her.

Ashley moaned into the mouth of her lover as her body shuddered in orgasm.

She couldn't believe what had happened; she had never had an orgasm with only her breasts being massaged before. It must have been her lovers' amazing tongues. The roughness made her body sensitive to their touch.

"Let me touch you," Ashley whispered, still feeling the aftershocks of her orgasm throughout her body. Kissing the hard male nipples of her first lover, she loved the sharp intake of his breath as she slowly kissed and licked her way down his body. Stopping when she reached the hard, thick length of his cock, Ashley looked up at him before she licked the head and the small bead of liquid sitting there.

Her second lover hadn't been forgotten as he followed her movements, kissing her neck and massaging her sensitive breasts as she fondled his mirror image.

Turning slightly, so she could both take the length of cock into her mouth and at the same time touch her second lover, Ashley set about enjoying herself. She loved the male groans of pleasure her lovers gave as she sucked one cock and stroked the other. She could happily stay like this for hours.

* * *

She had no time to remember anymore as she heard a voice calling to her.

"Come to us, Ashley. It is time. There will be no more hurt if you just open your eyes," said the voice.

The voices were getting harder and harder to ignore and she did want to see if they were just as beautiful when she was awake. The pain seemed to be easier somehow. Was it because she was contemplating joining them? Maybe she could try and see.

"I think we are breaking through the barriers she has put up in her mind. One more push and we should be in," she heard the voice say. It was a sexy sounding voice; she loved hearing it speak in her mind. Would it be like that when she was conscious? She hoped so, because it was pulling her out of the barren world and into the one it inhabited.

Chapter Four

Ashley slowly became aware of her surroundings. It was difficult to find the strength to open her eyes, so she lay still as she listened to the sounds of people talking. She didn't really follow what they were saying. Their conversation was just a noise in the background.

What is that delicious smell? Musky male with a hint of vanilla. How unusual. I wonder who it belongs to?

Ashley felt a dip beside her, then the brush of a hand on her head. The hand carefully moved some of her hair from her face, putting it behind her ear, then cupped her cheek in its large palm.

It brought the delicious smell closer to her. Ashley couldn't resist turning her face into the palm of the hand. She heard a deeply indrawn breath and felt the shudder that went through the body at her actions.

Was he one of the ones from her dreams?

Forcing her eyes to open, Ashley took a deep breath at the sight before her. A golden brown chest met her gaze; it looked like he had muscles upon muscles. She reluctantly pulled her eyes from his chest and looked upwards toward his face. The sight awaiting her caused her to forget breathing altogether.

She was so caught up in staring at his face that she was taken by surprise when the pallet on her other side depressed as someone else sat on it. Tearing her gaze from the face before her was hard, but she managed to turn her head slightly to see who else had joined them.

A second male sat beside her, staring deeply and hungrily at her; that was the only way to describe the look on his face. A mirror image of the first one, apart from the absence of a scar on his face -- had she noticed a scar on the first male?

Where was she? Who were these males who looked at her as though she were a dessert all prepared for their consumption?

Ashley watched as the golden god lifted his hand to touch her hair then move to her cheek. It was as though he could not believe she was there. She caught the same scent as before, musky male with vanilla undertones. Why did they smell the same? All thoughts were quickly forgotten as she remembered where she had seen them before. They were the men from her dreams.

"I know you both," she said as she turned back to the scarred one. "What are your names? Where am I?"

"I am Jarod, my mate. This is my brother Jeran."

"She has green eyes, Jarod."

Ashley turned to Jeran, who sounded winded when he spoke, as though he had been doing something energetic.

"Why does the colour of my eyes matter? Most Skylians have green eyes of one hue or another."

"We have been waiting for you to wake up so we could see the colour, Ashley. Now at last we can see them."

"The crash! Leah! Where is she? How long have I been out?" Ashley felt herself panic as she recalled arriving in the orbit of the planet they were to survey for the botanists of the base ship. She could recollect the system's failure and being unable to fasten herself into her safety harness properly, the way Leah had struggled to bring the ship into some sort of control, and then the snap of her bones as the shuttle crashed into a forest region. That was it, the last thing she remembered was shouting for help in her mind… and someone connecting with her briefly before she lost consciousness. But how was that possible?

Wait… her arm! She could move it all right. It wasn't broken now, but she was sure that it had been. "I remember breaking my arm as we crashed. Did Leah use our mediKit to heal it?" She knew she was rambling, not letting them answer her, but she was so worried something had happened to Leah she didn't want to hear bad news.

"Leah is well, my mate. It was you who were injured in the crash. With the help of Jarod and Jilla, I healed your broken bones, and today we managed to heal the rest of your injuries."

"Mate! You both said *my mate*. What do you mean? Why do you call me your mate?" Ashley looked from one to the other… waiting on an answer, knowing it was something she needed to hear.

What was that buzzing sound in her mind? It was as though a conversation was being held but she couldn't quite make out the words. Narrowing her eyes she studied the two males beside her. Were they telepathic? Were they talking to each other right now?

"What are you both saying to each other?" Ashley decided the only way to discover if her suspicions were correct was to ask. They both started and glanced at each other then at her, letting her know she was correct. They were a telepathic species… whatever they were.

"What planet is this and what species are you both?" She wanted answers and she wanted them now. And finding out where Leah was would be next.

"You are on the planet of Catari, Ashley. I am the Alpha of the Jageri people and Jeran is our Shaman."

"All right, thanks for that info. Now where is Leah?" Skyla, she was being rude, but not getting answers to her questions was making her cranky. She heard a sort of strangulated sound come out of Jarod when she said that. What, did no one speak to him that way?

I am the Alpha!

So what?

"Leah is with her mate. As you are with yours," Jarod replied.

Ashley felt the shiver run through her body at the way he growled out the words to her. Her pussy grew moist and her nipples tightened almost painfully in reaction. She looked away from him to Jeran, but that didn't help as she was looking at the same fascinating features. Skyla, more moisture was leaking from her pussy. What did he say? Leah was with her mate?

"Jason is here with a rescue party already? How long was I out of things?"

"No, little one, she is with Darius, the Alpha of the Leopai. It was on their territory that your ship crashed. We are their *guests* till you are well enough to travel home with us. Leah and Darius were joined as mates the day after the crash."

She felt a shudder of fear race through her at that news. Leah would never have agreed without a damn good reason. Did they hold her injuries over her head as an incentive? Was it her fault Leah was forced to mate with this Darius?

Ashley struggled to sit up; she had forgotten she was lying down looking like a helpless child. She wanted to make things more even and sitting up was better than lying there like an offering to the two of them. "What did you threaten her with to force her to mate with someone? I want to see her right away. I won't talk to you anymore till I see her for myself."

Ashley knew she was being stubborn, and maybe it was the wrong way to deal with these people, but she really needed the assurance that her friend was unharmed.

Jeran looked over at his brother helplessly at Ashley's words. Never did they think she would come to this conclusion. She was still struggling to sit up. He put a hand gently under her arm, saw Jarod do the same on her other side and helped. He fixed her pillows so that she could lean back, as just that little bit of exertion had tired her out.

Her scent hit him hard. His body reacted even more to her proximity than before, especially now that he had touched her as a mate and not as a healer. His cock felt like a steel poker and from Jarod's indrawn breath, he knew he was feeling the same.

Knowing that Ashley was fighting her own body's reaction to them wasn't helping him keep a clear head at all. The scent of her woman's juices overlaid with the mate scent of vanilla was driving him crazy. He needed to touch the beautiful raised nipples he could see through her sleeping gown. Agreement came from Jarod on their intimate link.

"Well! Go get Leah. Now!" Ashley said forcefully.

A growl came from deep in Jarod's chest at Ashley's words. Jeran knew he was keeping hold of his temper by a thread; he sought to defuse the tense lines of both in the only way open to him right now.

"I have contacted Jilla. She is letting Darius know you have awakened, my mate. Your friend will arrive soon."

"So you are a telepathic race. I thought you must be, but why could I not hear your conversation earlier? Skylians are telepathic although we don't use it with other species."

"We were using our intimate mind link, not the general one, but why you were able to know that I am not sure." Jarod looked over at Jeran.

I can only imagine it was because she connected with us when she was in danger. Combined with our healing link, she was able to tap into our intimate path. She is our mate and that will be the path we will use. Jeran was concerned; if she managed to connect clearly on that link, the mate link would automatically kick in before they could explain things to her. Then there would be no going back… for any of them.

Then we make sure she knows everything as soon as possible. She is going to learn not to have an attitude with me.

Jeran could only laugh inwardly at Jarod's words. He knew his brother would be waiting for the chance to put their mate in her place concerning what was acceptable behaviour and what was not.

"You're doing it again; I can hear the noise but not the words."

Jeran ran his finger down Ashley's arm and saw the reaction his caress had on her. Her eyes grew cloudy as she looked up at him; her nipples grew harder as they poked through her gown. He had to touch her.

Moving closer to her, Jeran softly kissed the point of her neck where it reached her shoulder. Hearing her gasp was worth the excruciating pain running through him at his proximity to her. He gently ran his tongue over the spot he had kissed, moving upwards to her beautiful little shell ear. He nibbled on the fleshy part of it, loving the catch in her breath as she felt his tongue swipe over to soothe the sting of his bite.

He was aware of Jarod moving closer, taking possession of her lips. He was so in tune with his brother that he felt his pleasure when she allowed him to touch her tongue with his. Heard both their gasps, at the desire coursing through their bodies… and through his.

Unfortunately they couldn't explore these feelings as the door to the room opened, drawing them apart.

Chapter Five

Ashley wondered what on Skyla she thought she was doing. One minute she was berating them, and the next letting them touch and kiss her. Both of them! Not just one, but both! Why was she reacting this way to them? Never had she felt such instant attraction to a man… or men in this case.

She focused on the door, and felt tears come to her eyes as Leah rushed through the opening, followed by a large male.

Ashley watched as her friend managed to find a way to move Jarod out of the way without touching him at all. Mind you, the rumble from the dark-haired male entering the room behind Leah might have had something to do with it.

"Oh, Ash, thank Skyla you are awake," said Leah. Ashley noticed her eyes were awash with tears.

"Lee, don't cry! I am fine," was all that she managed to say before she was enveloped in a tight hold. She felt tears come to her own eyes at seeing Leah was unhurt and looking well.

Pulling back from Leah, Ashley looked at her friend, just to make sure she hadn't missed any injury. She had to take a second look; she had never seen Leah look so… happy. Yes, that was the word; she was relaxed and glowing with health.

"What has been happening while I was unconscious? It looks like I missed a lot."

She watched Leah glance back at the dark-haired male, saw him come closer, but stop abruptly when Jeran growled low in his chest. What was it with these guys and their growling and snarling?

"I will leave you with your friend for a little while, Leah. I am sure you have things to discuss between yourselves."

Ashley knew that was a hint to Jeran and Jarod to leave the room too. She felt her heart give a lurch; she didn't want them to leave her alone! Skyla, had they brainwashed her? She wanted to talk to Leah to find out what had happened, but just the thought of them leaving her was… distasteful.

Looking from one to the other, she could see they didn't want to leave her. She also felt something else from them both, but how she did she wasn't sure. She could sense they were in -- pain? At that thought, Ashley remembered her dream in the barren place she had been. "Why are you in pain? What is causing it?" She noticed the looks the men gave her. "Stop talking between yourselves, and tell me what's going on."

Skyla, she was being curt again, but they were seriously starting to piss her off talking to each other so she couldn't hear them.

"It is all right, my mate; we will leave you with your friend. You will be hungry and once you have had food and rest we will come and explain everything to you," Jeran answered. He leaned down and gave her cheek a quick kiss.

She watched Jarod come around the bed pallet and repeat his brother's actions. Leah just sat there watching them with a smile on her face as though they had every right to take these liberties. Ashley watched Leah stand up and give the dark-haired male a quick kiss in farewell.

Once the three of them had left the room, Ashley turned her attention back to her friend, taking in more of the changes she could see. Oh they were slight, but Ashley had known Leah all her life. She could see that finally Leah was at peace with herself… and she could only guess at the cause of this happiness.

She noticed Leah was examining her with the same intensity. She had to laugh and was glad to see the answering one Leah gave her as she acknowledged that was what she was doing too. It felt good to be alone again… they needed to talk.

"How do you feel, Ash? I was in a short time ago, before Jeran started his healing. I am so glad to see you awake at last. I have been so worried about you."

"I am tired and a bit sore, but it's nothing compared to what I thought I would feel like. What has been happening while I was out of things?"

She watched the blush that started with Leah's face and travelled down her body. A body she could see quite clearly as she had on something that she would only have normally worn to sleep on their base ship. A short tunic, in a lovely shade of lilac.

"Um, well, a lot has happened in four days. After the crash, I met Darius and his men; they brought the two of us to their stronghold. This is the territory of the Leopai pack. You had serious head injuries. Mata, the Seer of the Leopai, could only start the healing process of your arm and other injuries. If Jeran hadn't arrived when he did, we might have lost you," Leah stated with a sheen of tears in her eyes.

Ashley reached out and took hold of her hand. "I am all right now."

"I thought I was going to lose you, Ash. The mediKit was broken. If Darius and his men hadn't found us…" Her voice trailed off as she swallowed. "Jeran and Jarod have been healing you for the last three days with the help of the Jageri Seer, Jilla."

"How have they been healing me? Do they have something similar to our mediKits?"

"No, Ash. The people here have amazing mental powers. Jeran is one of the strongest Shaman healers; he can take and use power donated to him by others. I wasn't allowed in to see him work, but I asked Aaron, our Shaman, about how healing works and he tried to explain things to me."

"Our Shaman?" It sounded as though Leah didn't think of herself as a Skylian anymore. She watched the bloom that came to Leah's face, the brightening of her eyes.

"Yes, Ash. I mean our Shaman of the Leopai. I -- I am mated with Darius, the Alpha of the pack, the man who came with me to see you."

"What about Jason? You are meant to mate with him when we return. Did they force you to mate so that I would be healed?" Ashley had to ask; the question had been eating away at her since Jeran told her that Leah had mated with Darius.

Leah looked back at her shocked. "No, of course they didn't force me. Why on Skyla did you think that, Ash?"

"It just seemed to fit. You always follow the rules, never break them… and this is a major breaking of rules! What else would I think?"

"I love Darius. I wouldn't have mated with him otherwise. He makes me feel… complete."

"It's just so sudden. I have never known you to act impulsively before. That is normally my behaviour. I am sorry to have come to the wrong conclusion." Ashley gave a little laugh. "At least now I know why Jarod was so pissed off with me. What is it with them and their growling anyway? I noticed Darius does it too."

"I -- I can't tell you, Ashley. Darius said that you had to hear things from Jarod and Jeran. But I can tell you that you have nothing to fear and a whole lot to gain."

"That's not like you, letting a male tell you what you are to do and say. Can't you tell me anything?" Ashley watched Leah closely as she nibbled her bottom lip.

"Well, I can remind you of what you said when we arrived in orbit of the planet. Think about it, Ash. What else had you dreamed about? If one thing is true, then what about the others?"

Ashley didn't have time to answer as the door opened and two females walked in, one carrying a tray with goblets, the other with plates of food. Leah stood up, smiling at them both, and turned back to her.

"This is Mata and Jilla, Ash. They are both Seers, and both had a hand in your recovery."

Watching the tall, beautiful women who came closer to her sleeping pallet, Ashley could tell who the Seer of the Jageri was; it had to be the one with dark blonde hair with streaks of gold running through it. Her eye colour and features were so like Jarod and Jeran. Mata, on the other hand, had long, black hair and blue eyes, similar to Darius, Leah's mate.

"We have brought you something to eat and drink. I put some herbs in the drink to help you sleep and some for the lingering pain you must be feeling," said Mata with a smile on her face.

Jilla put the tray she was carrying on the bedside table, and picked up one of the dishes. "We knew you wouldn't feel like something heavy right now, so we used some of our fowl eggs. Leah loves them; we hope you will too."

Feeling overwhelmed at the care and generosity these women were showing, not just to her but Leah, Ashley felt she had to try and eat something, although she wasn't really hungry, just thirsty. But they were right; she did feel better once she forced herself to eat some of the fluffy eggs and drank down the herb mix. It had a lovely citrus taste; she could do with more.

Taking the dish from her, Leah brushed back some of her hair from her face. "We will let you rest now, Ash. You look sleepy and when you wake up we will return to help you to the bathing room. You will feel much better after a good, long soak."

The three women helped settle her pillows and covers, making sure she was comfortable, and then left her to her dreams… dreams that featured two tall, golden men.

Chapter Six

Jarod wanted to return immediately to his mate's side when they came back from their run. He had experienced both relief at escaping the excruciating pain he felt in his mate's presence and not being able to claim her, and fear that she would again fall ill when he was not there to protect her.

"Jarod, Jeran, I was awaiting your arrival. Leah said Ashley was sleeping; she has had food and refreshment. Kara is keeping watch over her, and I wanted to talk to you before you returned to her side," said Darius as he stepped out of the shadows of the doorway.

Jarod looked over at his brother before shifting into his human form. Bones started to shift, and paws changed to legs and hands as their bodies morphed into men again.

"I know how hard it is for you both, wanting to claim your mate and being forced to wait on her recovery. I don't know if I would have had the strength to delay as you both have had to," Darius continued, taking a deep breath as he looked first at Jeran, then back to Jarod. "I know we haven't always agreed or even liked each other, but the situation has changed. My mate is friend to yours; I am willing to put aside all hostilities and ill feeling if you will do the same. I have found that I have to make my mate happy and content. She wouldn't be if she wasn't able to see her friend regularly."

Well, well, well. So Darius does have a soft spot after all.

Jarod acknowledged Jeran's comment with a slight nod. Fingering his scar, he noticed the grimace Darius gave at his action.

"I have to apologise for that scar. I didn't at the time and that was remiss of me. I hadn't intended to scar you. I have found since my mate's arrival things that seemed to matter before don't have the same significance anymore. We all will need to reevaluate our priorities."

This is the chance for lasting peace, my brother. He means what he says.

I know; I don't have to read his mind to see the truth in his words. It looks like you will be getting the harmony between our packs that you have been pressing for, Shaman.

With our mate being the close friend of the Pantheri leader, the time and circumstances could not be better, Alpha.

"I agree, Darius. Our packs have to be united in friendship and peace or our mates would not find it easy to meet with each other. I want Ashley to be able to visit her friend knowing she will be safe. I realise you must feel the same."

"So we are agreed; there will be settled peace between Jageri and Pantheri?"

"If you can guarantee all your Pantheri pack Alphas will follow the Leopai in peace, the Jageri will follow my lead. Blood oath, Darius."

Darius took his knife from the sheath at his side, slit a shallow cut in his left palm, and handed the knife to Jeran. Jarod took the proffered blade from his Shaman and used it to cut a similar wound in his left hand, then passed the blade back to Jeran.

"Clasp each other's hand," said Jeran as he laid the blade of the knife over their joined hands. Jarod watched as first the blade started to glow, then their joined hands. He noticed movement through the open doorway, and watched as Aaron and a young Leopai male came over and stood beside Jeran. He should have known Jeran would have called the local Shaman as further witness to their oath so there would be no ill will between Shamans to undermine the pact.

Jarod sensed the blood oath of comradeship and peace take hold of his being, knew from the grimace on Darius's face that he felt it too. Aaron laid his hand over Jeran's and the glow became brighter as the two Shamans sealed the oath. Nothing could break this pact between them now; not while both were as willing as they were to promote peace with each other.

"It is sealed and witnessed. There will be no further hostility between the Jageri and the Pantheri," confirmed Jeran and Aaron as they removed their hands and Jeran handed the knife back to Darius.

Looking at his hand, Jarod noticed all there was to show of the cut was a red scar. Jeran had healed the cuts before removing his hand. He didn't need to look at Darius's palm to know his would be healed too.

"I never expected to see this day. Thank you for calling us here, Jeran. It has put an old man's heart at ease to know that there will be lasting peace between our packs," Aaron said before taking the arm of his companion and leaving the three men alone again.

"I will leave you to return to your mate. I know that you are anxious to be with her," said Darius before he too turned and left them.

"You look pleased with yourself, Shaman."

"How can I not be, when everything that I have been pushing toward is imminent, Jarod? You know I have been telling you that we must all be of one mind if we are to survive what is to come. And no, I still don't know what it is, just that something tremendous is going to force all the packs to work together… or we will find that our lives will never be the same."

"Damn, I suppose that's what I get for having a brother who is a mystic. Only knowing so much and not the whole picture," Jarod complained with a shake of his head. "I need to be with my mate."

Jarod walked down the long corridor to the door of his mate's room. He looked at Jeran as they both took in the guards outside. Two Jageri and two Leopai, standing there in complete harmony of purpose, that of making sure that the Jageri Alpha and Shaman's mate was safe. It pleased him to see members of the two packs working together this way.

He gave the guards orders, then opened the door and asked the waiting Leopai woman to leave for the night.

Following his brother into Ashley's room, he breathed in her mate scent that held an undertone of pure womanly aroma, the perfume that was hers and hers alone.

Then the pain started.

"If we shift we will have more protection as the effects of not claiming her won't be as severe," Jeran suggested.

His body started to contort and change, his arms and hands morphing into legs and paws. He glanced over and saw Jeran had already shifted. Both turned and padded over to the side of the sleeping pallet.

Just watching Ashley as she slept brought more joy to Jarod than anything had previously in his life. He rubbed his nose along the length of Ashley's arm, then stepped back to allow Jeran to lay his scent on their mate. Both of them curled up on the floor, one facing the door, and the other facing the window, the room's only other entry point, and they settled down for the night. Nothing would get by them to reach their mate... not with both of them there to protect her.

* * *

Jarod woke up with a start. Jeran had been disturbed as well. Turning toward the pallet he saw Ashley twisting and turning in her sleep. He reached out with his mind, linking with his brother so that he could see what had distressed their mate.

She had to find her way out of here. It was so hot in the sun. Where were the two cats? They had helped her reach safety before; they would again. It was so barren, this desert she was lost in. If only she could remember what to call her cats, they would save her... she knew they would.

"What is she dreaming about, Jeran?"

"I think this is the place where she was trapped when she had her head injury. I recognise it from her memories. But why is she thinking about two cats? Does she know what we are without us having to tell her?"

"We have to go to her; she is frightened and alone. She needs us to bring her back again."

"Follow me -- and be careful. I will link the three of us mind to mind so that we know what she is thinking."

Chapter Seven

Ashley turned at the sound of footsteps coming toward her. She saw the two beautiful large cats of her dreams. Both were about eight feet in length, with muscular, stocky bodies. They were a brownish/yellow colour with dark rosette markings over their coats. She wasn't afraid of them. Although this was a different setting than the one she was used to seeing them in, she knew them.

"Why are you here? You have only come to me on our ship before. Who are you?"

Ashley moved closer, stopping a short distance from them and sitting down on the rocks. One of the cats lowered himself to the ground, and slowly slid on his belly one inch at a time till he was within touching distance.

When she didn't move back, or appear to be frightened, he moved closer, till he touched her hand with his nose. She jumped a little at the coldness, but didn't move her hand out of his reach. Taking this as a sign to go forward, the cat shifted till he had his head under her palm.

She drew in a deep breath, and then she gently ran her palm over the top of his head, back then forward. Purring started deep in his chest at her caress. She grew bolder and moved even closer to the large body that dwarfed her frame. Running her hand down over his head, neck and back she listened to the deep rumbles of pleasure. Out of the corner of her eye she noticed the second cat crawling closer, slowly, as though to let her know he wouldn't hurt her either.

He moved to her other side, butting his head against her arm, as though to say, "My turn now." Laughing in delight, Ashley turned her attention to the second cat, lightly rubbing his head, then neck. The first one lay his massive head down over her knees, watching her stroke his companion.

She wasn't sure how long she fondled them as she listened to the sound of their obvious pleasure at her touch, before she noticed that one of them had a scar on the right side of his face. It wasn't that she had been unobservant; the cat had deliberately kept that side of his face turned away from her till now.

Ashley gave a slight gasp at seeing the scar that looked so similar to Jarod's… in exactly the same place. She wasn't given a chance to assimilate this, as she just about jumped out of her skin when she felt the wetness and roughness of the other cat's tongue swipe across her breast.

She was shaken at its actions; the cat took full advantage and swiped his tongue over her nipple. Ashley was dazed at the deliberateness of its behaviour. It was as if it had been intentional and not just a general thank you gesture. She was taken aback even more when the second cat did exactly the same thing to the hard point nearest to him.

Ashley tried to move away from the two large bodies but the way they had her cornered between them made that difficult. She felt herself start to panic, then she remembered the scar. The second cat was watching her with an expectant expression on its face. She reached out and hesitantly touched the scar, and heard the purr in response.

"How do you have a scar so similar to the one Jarod has?" she asked as she looked into the amber-coloured eyes… eyes that looked so like his. Examining the first cat, she noticed the same coloured eyes returning her stare.

"This is weird. Now I am turning my dream cats into the two men I met today. I am seriously in need of help if I can't separate my real world from my dream one." Ashley saw the looks the two cats gave each other; you would think they understood her words and were working out what action to take. Not possible!

She was stunned when the two cats stood up and started to… shimmer, yes, shimmer. Ashley sat with her mouth open watching the unbelievable sight of the two cats shifting their form to become… Jarod and Jeran!

Ashley was speechless.

Jarod knelt down beside her, leaned closer and kissed her. Not a gentle peck on the cheek this time, but one that rocked her down to her feet. His tongue searched out hers and what a tongue it was. Rough, but oh so stimulating. She felt a gentle tug on the strap that held up her tunic as Jeran slipped it down her arm, baring her breast to his sight -- and touch. The warm mouth that covered her nipple felt oh so good, the nips from his teeth so stimulating. She felt the pleasure travel down to her womb. Jarod finished his kiss and moved back, slipping the strap nearest him down, to expose both breasts this time.

"Lie back, my mate. Let us pleasure you," Jeran commanded, as both of them pulled her tunic down over her body, waiting till she was lying flat to manoeuvre it over her hips, revealing her body to their gaze.

She felt so exposed lying there before them, but was unafraid. She knew they would never hurt her. She had somehow always known that.

"You are beautiful, my mate. Jeran, look at those hard, red nipples. They are just waiting for our touch."

"Stunning, but I am going taste this little pussy that smells so enticing," said Jeran, as he slid between her legs, pushing them apart till he got his shoulders between them, then licked her pussy.

Ashley was awash with sensation. Jeran's nibbles on her clit and that amazing abrasive tongue he slid into her waiting centre caused more of her feminine liquid to flow. From his growl he was enjoying her taste. Jarod attached himself to her taut bud, sucking strongly but not painfully, just enough pleasure to make her moan and move restlessly against Jeran's mouth, wanting more attention on her clit. Jarod fondled her other nipple as he drew on the one in his mouth then moved to her other leaving a damp trail of moisture as he licked his way to her waiting nubbin.

Ashley loved the attention she was getting from them both, but she wanted to take an active part. After all, this was her dream. She should be able to decide who touched who -- and where.

"I want to touch you both," she said, watching their heads lift. She drew in a deep breath and tried to move away from their touch. "Skyla, your eyes are glowing," she whispered as she looked from one to the other, watching as their eyes changed colour from their normal amber to a golden hue, then back.

Ashley fought her way to full consciousness. She remembered the warm mouths on her nipples and clit, the way her dream men had made her wet with desire. She opened her eyes when she heard a rustling sound, turned her head on the pillow… and looked at the two large cats from her dreams.

How can this be? Ashley sat up on her sleeping pallet.

She should be frightened out of her wits, but if her dream was any indication, she had nothing to fear from them.

"Why -- why are you here? How did you get in my room?" Ashley asked as she did something her people frowned on. But then, when had she ever followed rules? She reached out with her mind to see if she could get any surface thoughts from her visitors, beginning to wonder if her dreams were more than that.

Chapter Eight

Jeran watched his mate as she registered their presence. He was amazed that she wasn't afraid of them, that she hadn't shouted for help at seeing them beside her pallet.

She is exactly what we need, brother. She has always known us deep in her subconscious, Jarod said.

Before Jeran could respond, to his alarm, he felt the delicate brush on his mind. Ashley was attempting to mind link with them! On the very intimate link that the three of them would share when mate linked.

No! Jeran roared, knowing in his heart that he was too late to stop Ashley from setting their mate link in place. He should have anticipated her actions and made sure she knew what would happen if she ever attempted to link with them both on the path she had discovered earlier that day.

Jeran started his change, limbs and paws transformed to legs, arms, hands and feet. He knew Jarod was doing the same. They would be too late to stop the very thing they both wanted, but they had to give Ashley a choice. Jeran sat on the edge of the pallet and took a shivering Ashley into his arms. "It's all right, my mate. You were aware of who we were, even though you tried to deny it."

Jarod moved to her other side, stroking her shoulders gently. Then he felt the stirring of the mate link taking hold.

"What is happening to me -- to us?" Ashley asked as she looked up at him.

"You have set our mate link in motion. We wanted to give you the choice in this, but it is too late. Nothing can stop this now," Jarod replied.

Jeran saw Ashley's eyes grow wider as she too felt the strands grow from the little corner of her mind that waited for this very occasion. He watched as the strands moved closer to his mind, attaching themselves to the place that held his link with Jarod. Observed as they grew thicker and reinforced his link with his brother into something stronger, more intimate than before, then looked and saw how the strands made their own path into a corner of Ashley's mind to complete the circle.

He looked deep into Ashley's eyes, knowing she saw the strands grow and multiply, then glow in a glistening gold.

"I -- I can feel you both, in my mind. Not just there, all over me. Why were you in so much pain? Thank Skyla it's easing now. How could you stand it?"

"It was because we were unable to fully claim you as our mate. We decided you should learn about us first, about our people -- and then we would give you the choice to join with us as our mate," Jarod answered.

"But you were in such pain! Why didn't you just join us together? I wouldn't have blamed you. Not with the pain you were both in."

Jeran looked over at Jarod, hardly believing Ashley's reaction. He had expected many things but not this acceptance of them.

Do you think she is still concussed and is not taking in the seriousness of this?

Before Jeran could answer, Ashley sighed and shook her head. "You do realise that I can hear you and comprehend everything you say on the link now?"

This is going to take some getting used to! They were accustomed to communicating privately, but now they would have to take their mate into account. "I am sorry, my mate," Jarod said hesitantly. "I will try to remember you can hear me when I communicate with Jeran."

Ashley turned back toward Jeran, rolling her eyes as she did. "Is he always so serious?"

Jeran let out a short laugh. He was looking forward to seeing how much leeway Jarod would let Ashley have before he let her know his limits. She was exactly what his oh so serious brother needed.

"Hey, what was that for?" Ashley jumped, rubbing the side of her neck.

"I don't appreciate being laughed at," Jarod growled at her.

"It was a joke, something to lighten things. I -- it's how I cope, Jarod. You have to realise I have a lot of questions and if I didn't act this way I would be crying my eyes out right now." Ashley turned her gaze back to Jeran.

Jeran gathered her gently into his arms, giving her the comfort she needed. He watched Jarod close his eyes and take a deep breath before burying his face into Ashley's neck, licking the small red area from the nip he had given her a few moments earlier.

"I am sorry, my mate," Jarod said in remorse, in between licks to Ashley's neck.

Jeran felt the shudder that ran through her body as Jarod's touch started to affect her. Her nipples were hard points against his chest and he knew they had to stop before things got out of control. She needed answers first.

"Jarod, you have to stop. Ashley is right; she does need answers now."

Growling, Jarod pulled away from Ashley, and looked back at Jeran. "You are correct, brother, as much as I wish you weren't."

"Little one, we will try to answer all your questions, just let us move over to the chairs by the fireplace," Jeran said as he reluctantly moved his body away from his mate.

"I can't believe how intense it is, having your feelings and thoughts running along with mine. What I felt was strengthened by your reaction, making it hard to deny what my body feels when you both hold me." Ashley's body shuddered with arousal.

Jeran plucked Ashley from her bed, cradling her in his arms, and carried her over to one of the lounging chairs, making sure she was comfortable before moving to sit on the one remaining beside Jarod. His cock beneath his loincloth was like a steel rod. He was sure Jarod was experiencing the same discomfort as he was.

He watched as Ashley looked from his brother to him and back again, biting her lip as she worked out in her mind what she wanted to ask them. He should take pity on her and just tell her, but he enjoyed the hot glances she was throwing his way.

"You told me before that you were Jageri, and Leah said that this was the Leopai land. I take it that the people here can also turn into cats?"

"Yes, that is correct; they turn into a different type of cat than we are," Jarod confirmed.

"Tell me about the mate link," Ashley requested quickly.

Sighing, Jeran focused his thoughts on how to explain to Ashley how and why she was now tied to them both.

"When a Catari male first encounters his mate, they realise right away they are mates, and it is instinctual to want to link minds with each other. Even if the actual physical joining is delayed, the mind link is normally immediate. But you were injured when we met you. You are also not of Catari, so we made the choice to wait till you were healed so that you could learn more about us and our people first," Jeran explained as he searched for a way to answer the questions that were bubbling up in her mind.

"What caused the pain I know both of you were feeling? Was that because the mate link was not in place?" Ashley asked.

"It was painful for us to be near you and not have a link with you. You are the other half of my soul, the one I -- we -- have been waiting for our whole life. Both of us needed to link with you, to join our minds. It would have been unfair of us to do this without your consent. We could not force this on you, even though it was our first and second thought to do just that."

"Leah told me it took days for you to heal me. How did you both stand it when you were in such debilitating pain?"

Jeran saw Jarod clench his fists together on his thighs, in an attempt to stop from leaping to his feet and going over to their mate. He didn't blame his brother one iota. He wanted the very same thing -- to have her safe in their arms. Who held her didn't matter, as long as one of them did.

"Why do your people need a mind link with your mates? How can this be so important to you?" Ashley asked.

"It is important as it keeps the males grounded. We are a race of predators, and our mates keep us from going wild. It is hard enough when we are alone, but when a mate enters our lives nothing and no one can be allowed to harm her. We need to touch the minds of our mates once we meet them. To not have this is agonising to a Catarian. Once the link is in place we would be aware of each other all the time. You would just have to think of me and you would know where I was and what I was doing. I think you are already aware of this aspect. I know it is unsettling for you right now, but we have longed for this moment. Once we know that you are content, we will not be such a visible presence in your mind."

"Maybe you won't be, but I like this just fine," growled Jarod.

Jeran had to agree with him, as he had no intention of budging even the slightest inch from her mind. But he was trying to calm her, not make her more edgy. "To answer your first question, it was hard, but you are our mate. We needed to make you well again. No discomfort would stop us from achieving that goal."

"But why not just join us when it would have made healing me easier on you both?"

"We made the decision to give *you* the choice of joining with us, my mate. No matter the cost in discomfort, we would never have changed our minds on that. We are not savages to take that choice from you," Jarod snarled as he stood up to put another log on the fire.

Jeran saw the indrawn breath Ashley took as she watched Jarod fighting to keep control of his emotions. She stood up and walked up to him, running her palm gently over his shoulder and arm. Jeran had to fight not to go to them both; this was something Jarod had to deal with himself.

"I know you are not a savage, Jarod. I was just curious about why you never took that option," Ashley said as she moved closer to Jarod, close enough that she could lay her head on his shoulder.

"Why are you taking this so well? Why have you not run screaming from the room after all that has gone on between us?" Jeran asked, as Jarod turned around, drawing a willing Ashley into the comfort and protectiveness of his arms.

Pulling away from Jarod, Ashley looked over at Jeran. "Apart from my dreams about the two of you, I am taking this so well, as you put it, because of one thing and one thing only. Leah."

"What has Leah to do with your acceptance of us, my mate?" Jarod asked as he lifted Ashley into his arms and sat down on the chair with her on his knee.

"I have known Leah all my life. She is only a few months older than I am. We have always been friends, and earlier, for the first time since we were children, I saw her happy and content."

"Seeing her happy was enough for you to accept everything about us?" said Jarod as he stroked Ashley's hair.

"You probably think it silly, but yes. Oh, how to tell you my reasons. Leah is -- was -- the daughter of the commander of our base ship. She hardly had a childhood because of that. She was brought up with all the expectations of having a commander as a father. Never being able to just be herself! The only time she rebelled -- if you can call it that -- was when her intended mate arrived from one of the other base ships. She managed to get permission to hold off the joining, made the excuse that she wanted more time to get to know Jason, and that she wanted to have a joint ceremony with me. At no other time, apart from being irritated that she would have to stop flying when joined, has she gone against any of the rules and regulations."

Ashley took a deep breath before continuing, "To see her glowing like she was today, well, if Darius managed to break through all her worries and concerns and she accepted him, then I know that I don't have to be frightened of you two."

Jeran couldn't sit without touching her any longer. He reached over for her hand and brought it to his lips. Giving the palm a kiss, then a lick, he felt her move her hand till she was cradling his cheek in her palm. Her scent was driving him insane with need, but from her thoughts he knew she was exhausted. Looking over her head to Jarod he saw the same awareness of their mate in his eyes.

Jarod stood up, still cradling Ashley in his arms, and moved over to the sleeping pallet. After laying her down he started to cover her with the sheet when she caught his hand and tried to pull him down toward her.

"Stay with me. Both of you stay and hold me," Ashley said, covering her mouth as she yawned.

Jeran moved to her other side, and sat down beside her. "Don't you need to sleep, mate? You are exhausted by everything that has happened tonight."

"I need both of you to hold me. Please."

Jeran didn't need a second invitation, and knew that Jarod didn't either. He slid into bed beside Ashley, turning away from her so she could cuddle up behind him. No other thought went through his mind as he fell into a deep sleep, content for the first time in days.

Chapter Nine

Ashley slowly came awake as she realised the warm bodies of her mates had left the bed. *Mates*! How did she really feel about the events of last night? What she said to them both was true; she wouldn't have taken things so easily if she hadn't seen the glow of happiness on Leah's face. Still, she was fighting to keep calm when they weren't close to her. Somehow being with them, all her worries disappeared, but alone -- they all came clamouring to the front of her mind.

Their personalities were totally different. Jarod was pure Alpha in his attitude; he would show no compromise in a relationship. She supposed that Jarod was as he was because of the responsibility of leading his people. His gruffness sent sparks through her body when he showed his irritation to her. Yes, he would be so much fun to tease.

Jeran came across as much more compassionate and willing to give and take. But she knew that he also was an Alpha male, just one not afraid of showing his tender side. She had a feeling that he was constantly misread by people who didn't know him, and they would find out to their cost if they did something that displeased him. His gentleness to her, his willingness to heal her and need to take care of her -- she had never had that before. Not to the extent he wanted to take it.

Are you all right, my mate?

Do you need us, Ashley?

Ashley gave a start at the two distinctive voices in her mind. It amazed her that she had no trouble identifying who asked which question. Jeran wanted to know if she needed them, and Jarod claimed her as his mate.

I am all right, just thinking.

How do you feel this morning?

I feel tired, but otherwise so much better than when I woke up yesterday.

Ashley broke off her conversation with Jeran as the door to the room opened and Leah popped her head around. Smiling when she saw that Ashley was awake, she opened it wider and walked into the room with Jilla following her with a goblet in her hand.

I will let you talk with your friend. If you need us we are just a thought away.

She felt their presence fade from the forefront of her mind, but she could tell they were hovering at the back, out of sight but still there.

Ashley returned the hug Leah gave her.

"You look so much better this morning, Ash. Jilla has some more of the tonic, and we thought you would feel better if you had a bath, then had something filling to eat. Did you sleep all right?" Leah sat beside her on the bed, only moving slightly back when Jilla passed Ashley the citrus drink.

Taking a slow sip of the potion, Ashley wondered how to tell Leah about the events of the night. "Well, I had an unusual dream again, similar to the ones I had on the base ship." Ashley knew Leah would know the ones she referred to.

"Um, Ash, I know that you have mate linked with Jeran and Jarod; they were talking about it with Darius. I sort of overheard, but what I want to know is if you are happy with things."

"It was a bit frightening when it started. I wondered what was going on, but Jeran explained what had happened."

"Wait. What do you mean he explained what had happened? Why didn't he explain before he set the link in place?" Leah demanded in an agitated voice.

"They didn't set the link in place, Leah, I did. Remember yesterday when I said I could hear sound but not their words when they were talking together? Jeran said that with the healing they did, and with me being their mate, the path he used for healing was the same as the mate link. They were going to explain things to me today, but I sort of reached for both of them with my mind when I woke up after my dream and found the two of them sitting by my bed. They were in cat form then and I wanted answers."

"Oh, Ash. I wish you could have had the choice as I did," said Leah.

Ashley reached for her friend's hand, hating to see tears in her eyes, especially for something she couldn't have done anything about. Well, she could have told her about them being cats.

"Leah, I am really all right with it. Well, I am when they are both with me. It's when I am alone that doubts come into my head." Ashley turned to Jilla. "Can you tell me anything else that might have been missed? I know that they would have kept you up to date with everything, Jilla."

"Yes, my Alpha. They went to talk to Darius, as he is the Alpha here. Both Jarod and Jeran would like to ask Aaron to perform the mating ceremony here before we go back to our pack. Normally Jeran, as Shaman, performs the joining, but he wouldn't be able to do this for himself. His apprentice is not advanced enough to do this either, so as we now have a friendship pact with the Leopai, they thought this would be a goodwill gesture. Plus it will allow your friend to witness the ceremony."

Ashley held up her hand to prevent any further information. She wanted to find out what a *mating ceremony* consisted of. "What do you mean we need to have a ceremony? I thought we were mated already with the mate link?" Ashley felt confused by the different rules of this society.

Jilla shook her head. "No, the mate link is just the first step, one that is normally set in place immediately after a pair recognises themselves as mates. Then there is the ceremony that the Shaman performs, which joins you to each other in ways that are unbreakable."

"So are you telling me the link we have can be broken, if I decide I want to return home when the search party comes for us?" Ashley felt the instant denial flowing through the link she shared with Jarod and Jeran. She hated to be the cause of the pain that streamed through her thoughts at her question, but she needed to know.

White-faced at her question, Jilla answered, "I -- I think you need to talk to your mates, Alpha."

"All right."

Well, are you going to answer me? I know you are both there.

Jarod answered her first. *We will never let you leave us, mate. You belong with us now.*

Ashley heard Jeran's sigh and the pain that ran through him as he answered. *The link can be broken at this stage. If that is your wish we would not force you to stay with us.*

Jilla gave a gasp at his words. "No."

Jarod, do you agree with Jeran, that I can leave if I wanted to?

She heard his quiet answer with wonder in her heart. *Yes, we could never keep you with us if it would make you unhappy.*

Ashley turned to look at Jilla. "Why did you say *no* when Jeran said the link can be broken?"

"I -- I -- please, Alpha. You don't know what will happen if the link is severed now," Jilla said in a panicked tone.

"That is what I am trying to find out, Jilla. Now tell me," Ashley demanded with growing impatience.

"Once a link is set, it can never be totally broken. If you were to leave they would never be able to function without the touch of your mind now that they have felt it. You yourself would find it hard, but I don't know if it would be any more than that as you are not of Catari. But my Alpha and Shaman would not survive without you."

Enough, Jilla.

No, Jarod, I had to know if you would give me the choice to leave. I just didn't realise the implications it would have on both of you, which is why I asked Jilla to explain things to me.

Ashley turned to Leah who was as white-faced as Jilla. Shaking her head at her friend, she said, "Well, I got my choice in the end, Leah."

She was unable to bear the pain still flowing through the link any longer. *I am your mate for now and for as long as you want me. I needed to know that you would let me go if I wanted, but it was only a question. Not something I would have asked of you.*

The wave of relief that came from all sides hit her hard enough to make her eyes water.

We are coming to see you…

No, don't. I need a bath and some food. Jilla can fill me in on the ceremony. I take it you have that organised for today?

Yes, Aaron is most happy to have been asked to perform it for us. Are you sure you don't need us there?

I am fine. I take it this ceremony is going to be nothing like I have seen before? Oh, it's all right, don't answer that. I can see from the quick image from your mind that it's going to be an eye opener.

Ashley glared at her friend. "You could have warned me about the ceremony yesterday."

We will see you later, my mate.

Call if you need to ask us anything else.

Leah hugged her tightly. "Why should I warn you when it was a surprise for me?" she said and burst out laughing.

* * *

Ashley felt clean and fresh now that she was bathed and dressed again. Looking down at the tunic Leah had lent her, she shook her head at the briefness of it. But the freedom of movement it gave and the coolness from the heat of the day made her realise that this was the dress of necessity for these people. Anything else would be far too unpleasant to wear.

The bathing room had been an experience for her. Thankfully she hadn't needed the attendant's services to remove her pussy hair. But from Leah's flushed cheeks Ashley could imagine the shock it had given her system to have had that done.

The central dining area was massive, not that there were many people around right now, only a few of the older women who served them some food. Jilla had things she had to coordinate for the ceremony so she had left them after they bathed.

"I know there are things you need to ask, Ash, but it really would be better coming from your mates. Darius wouldn't tell me much about what was going to happen. I supposed he was frightened I would run," Leah said with a giggle.

Ashley stared at her. Leah giggling? She shook her head and said with a grin, "I love the way you have changed, Lee. It's obvious that Darius is good for you."

"Oh, he is good for me all right. Any more good and I wouldn't be able to walk."

"Leah, I am shocked." Ashley couldn't help the answering giggle as both of them convulsed into laughter. It felt good to be so at ease with her friend. She hadn't realised how uptight Leah had become with the arrival of Jason.

That thought brought Keevan, her own intended mate, to mind. Eyes clouding, Ashley said, "What will Keevan think of this? I don't want him to be hurt, but what else will he be when I say I am staying here?"

Leah put her hand over hers. "I know it's going to be hard, and I am not looking forward to a confrontation myself. But there is no way I could or in fact would go back to the base ship. I am free to be myself here. I would never return."

"Keevan has always been more of a friend -- to both of us. I just want him to be happy." Ashley broke off as she saw Jilla and Mata come through the door and head toward their table.

"Everything is prepared for the ceremony; all that is needed is for you to put on your gown," Jilla said.

"Oh, I thought I was to wear this one."

"Jageri mates wear a different colour gown for the ceremony. I asked some of the same women who made Leah's gowns if they could quickly make one for you. It is in your room, come." Mata turned toward the door.

Ashley looked at Leah, who shrugged and gave a small smile. Oh well, when in Catari do as the Catarian do.

Chapter Ten

Jeran nudged Jarod's arm to bring his attention on the gathering women who parted to allow them their first glimpse of their mate since reluctantly leaving her side that morning. The long hours since Jarod saw her warm and safe had made functioning difficult. But to see the results of the pampering Ashley had received more than made up for any discomfort her absence caused.

She looked beautiful in the traditional colours of the Jageri -- a pale, leaf green tunic made especially for her by the women of the Leopai. The colour brought out the gorgeous and unusual green shade of her eyes.

Jarod watched her reaction to the sight of them standing beside the Leopai Shaman, waiting for her to join them. But he would not allow her to walk that distance by herself. They murmured apologies to Aaron for deserting him and walked quickly to their mate's side.

The women drifted away from her side as they approached, till only her friend remained. They watched as Leah gave Ashley a quick kiss before leaving her standing there alone. Not taking her eyes off them she moved forwards, meeting them partway.

Jarod took her hand gently in his. "You are beautiful, my mate."

Jeran's silent agreement from Ashley's other side flowed through their mate link.

"Aaron is going to perform the ceremony, Ashley. If you have any concerns, please ask us on our link. We will try to alleviate your worries," Jeran murmured as the three of them moved toward the altar in front of the crowd of Jageri and Leopai who had come to witness a second joining in the space of a week.

There are so many people here; I didn't expect it.

We had a pleasant surprise when we spoke to Darius this morning. He had contacted his men guarding our people on the boundary, and gave them permission to come and join us. Fifty of our pack are here to witness our joining. When we return home, we will have a celebration for our people who have missed this day.

As Jarod listened to Jeran explaining events to Ashley, he still found it hard to believe the trust Darius was now showing to him and his pack. All that had happened before was wiped out by the arrival of two petite women!

"Ashley, this is Aaron, the Shaman of the Leopai. He has agreed to join the three of us today," said Jeran.

"It is good to meet you, Ashley. I am delighted to have been asked to perform this joining ceremony," Aaron said, as he took her hand in his and led her nearer the altar, until she was facing the assembled group.

Jarod moved to Ashley's right side, and followed his brother's movement as Jeran moved to her left.

"Jarod, Jeran and Ashley are here to be joined as mates," Aaron told the waiting crowd.

Aaron turned to face them. "Jarod, take Ashley's right hand and Jeran, take her left in yours." The Shaman picked up two lengths of cording from the altar and bound their hands together. He turned back toward the altar, lifted the ceremonial stole and placed it over his shoulders, then lifted a jewelled dagger. "Jarod, Jeran, will you say the joining words to Ashley?"

Jarod gazed deeply into Ashley's beautiful green eyes. Jeran said the words of joining with him. "I claim you as my mate. I will protect and care for you, cherish and love you until the day I die. I take you as my mate, never to be separate again."

Jarod felt a pull on his heart as they waited for Ashley's words to be spoken in return. They knew she would find the words she needed to say from their thoughts.

"I accept you both as my mates. I will love and care for you, cherish and stand by your side till the day I die. I take you as my mates, never to be separate again."

As Ashley spoke, the tension that had built snapped, the pressure eased, and Jarod found himself joined even deeper with her than he had been before. The peace he felt was amazing; to know she felt the same made the long days waiting for her to awaken worthwhile.

Aaron cut the cord from their wrists, then took Jarod's hand and made a shallow cut on his palm. He turned to Ashley, took her hand and made a shallow cut on her palm. As gentle as Aaron had been, Jarod knew from her sharp intake of breath that it had stung. And that was only the first cut.

He watched as Aaron brought their cut palms together and tied them with another cord. He then turned to Jeran so that he could repeat the whole event with him and Ashley.

From the pale look on her face she just realised that she would have to go through the whole thing again. He heard the whispered encouragement Jeran gave her through their link, and watched the relieved look on her face.

"The joining words have been spoken. The mingling of blood is complete. All that remains is the physical joining of your bodies."

Ashley gave a jump at the cheer that rang out from the waiting crowd. He moved his body slightly to the side so that his people could see their Alpha female clearly.

"What did the mingling of blood do?" Ashley whispered.

"It helps to complete the joining; it will aid with the transformation you will now go through," Jarod answered her quietly, waiting to see what her reaction would be.

"Transformation? What transformation? You never mentioned this before," Ashley gasped out, looking from one to the other.

Jeran said, "You will become like us, Ashley, a Jageri."

"Why didn't you tell me before this?" demanded Ashley. Then she gave a shiver as he filled her mind with the pleasures the three of them could look forward to in their cat form. "Oh!"

Aaron untied the cord from their wrists and placed his own palms over their cuts. A tingling heat ran through Jarod's hand and up his arm, spreading through his upper body. He could see from Ashley's reaction she was feeling the same. He licked his lips as he saw her nipples harden into tight kernels that strained through the tunic.

Having healed his and one of Ashley's hands, Aaron moved to perform the same service to Jeran. As he watched Ashley's breathing become more strained, he found it was impossible for him not to move closer and kiss her. She looked up at him, eyes clouded with desire, and lifted her face, lips straining to join with his.

He knew Aaron moved away from the three of them once he healed the cuts, but all Jarod was concerned with was claiming his mate. He put his hands on Ashley's shoulders and pulled her closer to him. Jeran moved so that she was caught between the two of them.

Jeran could hardly believe the sensations that had taken over his body. Oh, he knew, in theory, what happened when mates were joined, but the reality was so much more intense than mere words could express.

Nibbling on Ashley's neck wasn't enough for him; he had to see more of her body. Unfastening the ties at her shoulders he let the loose fabric slide down to expose her lovely back to his gaze and touch. The catch of Jarod's breath as he moved his hands around Ashley's body and cupped her breasts in his hands, offering them to his brother, sent a flash of sensation through his body right to his groin.

Pinching the nipple of one breast while his brother feasted on her other, he kissed his way down her neck and back up, gently nibbling and sucking at the spot he would soon claim as his.

The aroma coming from Ashley's pussy was overwhelming. His body was demanding he taste her sweet juices. Impatiently he dragged the tunic over her hips, helped by Jarod who took the opportunity to move to the nipple Jeran had been teasing.

Growling, Jeran moved round to the front of Ashley and stared at the beautiful sight of her lovely, moist labia, bare as a Jageri female should be. He sniffed the arousing scent of her pussy and moved close enough to run his tongue over the edges of her folds. The shudder that ran through Ashley's body told him she enjoyed that brief touch. Purring, he moved her legs wider so he could reach his objective more easily.

Parting her lovely flushed pink folds, Jeran swiped his tongue from top to bottom, enjoying the tangy yet sweet taste of her juices. The gasp she gave and the relaxing and widening of her legs pleased him. Linked as he was, he knew that Jarod was enjoying feasting on her breasts, stimulating them so that she produced even more of her sweet woman's liquid for him to drink.

His tongue entered her centre and moved back and forwards, in and out, simulating the action that his cock would take in a short time. It would have to be short, because much more of this stimulus and he would waste his seed in his loincloth. A murmur of agreement from Jarod told him he was near his limit in endurance. It was no surprise really; all he had to do was look at Ashley and want to be inside her.

"I want to touch you both. Let me pleasure you as you pleasure me."

Hearing Ashley's words, Jeran knew that he could wait no longer. Stepping back, he let Jarod take over.

"Go down on your hands and knees, mate. I have to get inside you now," Jarod demanded.

Jeran loved the hazy and passion-filled gaze Ashley gave him before looking at Jarod. Licking her lips, she ran a finger over Jarod's chest, moving from one hard male nipple to the next. "All right, but promise that I get to touch you soon."

Jarod whipped off his loincloth, and then gently pushed on her shoulders until she was on her hands and knees facing Jeran.

Jeran thought he had the best position for now; he was going to feel her perfect mouth on his cock. Releasing the ties on his loincloth, he saw the deep breath his mate took as she gazed at his steel hard cock staring her right in the face.

"Touch me, my mate. I need your touch," whispered Jeran. The feel of her small hand grasping his length nearly unmanned him; the sensations of pleasure drew up his sac tight against his body. He needed something to distract him from shooting his seed into her face. When he came for the first time, he intended to be deep within her pussy.

Jarod had not wasted any time. He was busy nibbling and kissing his way down Ashley's spine. As Jeran looked at his brother's flushed face he knew that he was not going to last long either. Both had waited for this moment for years it seemed. The feel of his cock being taken into the warm depths of Ashley's mouth brought him back to his own pleasure. She could only manage to take the tip of him into her mouth, but the nibbling bites and licks she gave the crown were much better than if she had been able to take more of him deeper.

The moans she made as she licked her way from tip to root led him to believe she enjoyed herself. *Of course I am enjoying myself, Jeran. I wouldn't be letting myself be this exposed to everyone if I wasn't.*

The sound of Ashley's mind voice sent a shiver through him, and he wasn't surprised to see pre-come leak from the tip of his cock. Hearing Ashley purr when she saw the bead of liquid, and the resultant lick she took, sent a shudder through their mate link. Jarod growled and Jeran saw the grip he had on Ashley's hips as he waited no longer to enter his mate's body.

Ashley felt as though she were a passenger in her own body; the way these two golden gods were pulling all reservations from her was a revelation. She forgot the people looking on. They were nothing to her. All that mattered at this moment was the pleasure of her mates' touch. She had no uncertainties. This was meant to be. The dreams she'd had of them, both in their human and cat forms, had led her to this moment. They'd been right. She had always known them. Deep down she knew that the dreams had been preparing her for this moment for months. Later she would have to ask Jeran how he had done it -- given her dreams of them, because he could be the only one who could have arranged them.

She felt Jarod's cock at the entrance of her pussy, gently pushing then retreating till with a snap the head of his cock made it past the elastic sheath of her entrance. Gasping at the unexpected sting as the thickness of his member entered her, Ashley moved her hips back, encouraging him to fill more of her waiting depths. His fingers gripping her hips grew almost painful then with a surge he filled her with his length.

"Skyla! More, Jarod, I want more," she gasped around Jeran's cock. Giving it one last lick, she closed her eyes as the sensations of pleasure ran through her body as Jarod's movements sped up. Jeran caught her face in his hands and brought her lips to his, biting and nibbling then kissing her with passion. At the same time Jarod fucked her with fervour. Tearing her mouth from Jeran with regret as Jarod pulled her back against his chest, she felt the warm sensation of her impending orgasm flush her entire body. Jarod licked the side of her neck then just as her orgasm took over, he sank his teeth into the tender skin, sucking and licking her blood. His own orgasm shook his body, and jets of seed shot into the waiting depths of her pussy. The sensation of the warm sucking mouth at her neck sent her spiralling into another orgasm.

A panting, sweat soaked Jarod rested his head against her neck. Jeran kissed his way down to her nipples and gently sucked them, as though to soothe her. Her body trembled with the force of her reaction to both the frantic fucking and the blood taking. It all seemed so amazing to her that they wanted her with them so badly they would physically alter her body so she could bear their young. Oh, she looked forward to that day with anticipation.

Jarod pulled away from her, withdrawing from her body. She let him go reluctantly, but knew that the ceremony was not over yet, as Jeran still had to join with her. She was such a lucky woman! “Mate, I am sorry I have harmed you!” Jarod said in a shaken voice.

“What? You didn’t hurt me, Jarod. I loved…”

“I have marked your body. I didn’t realise I was gripping you so hard. Forgive me, my mate.”

Ashley looked back at him, noticing he was staring shakily at the bruising appearing on her hips where he had gripped her in his passion. Shaking her head, Ashley said, “Jarod, I bruise easily. You did not hurt me. I loved the way you made love to me, your roughness along with the tenderness. Please believe me when I say if it wasn’t for the fact that I want Jeran, I would be begging you to fuck me again.”

Seeing the proud and arrogant look that came over Jarod’s face, Ashley knew she had said the right thing. She would never let this man think he had hurt her when it wasn’t true. She loved his arrogant attitude. Not that she wouldn’t enjoy the odd occasion of goading him into losing his temper. She had an idea that his idea of revenge would be body shaking pleasure… for both of them.

“You must be sore though, as I was not gentle, and I am not exactly small. We have a tradition among the Jageri of making sure our mates are properly cleansed after claiming. This has the added benefit of healing any soreness we might have caused during lovemaking.” Jarod grinned before ducking his head down between her legs and licking her pussy from top to bottom and back. His rough tongue sent shudders through her body, and her legs opened wider as he pushed his face closer.

“Skyla!”

Ashley was amazed at the sensations running through her body. She didn't think she would be able to keep up with them. But the more they touched her the more she needed. Once Jarod reduced her to a limp rag, Jeran took his place behind her. The gentle touch of his hands running over her hips brought instant calm. The sensation of the blunt head of his cock at her entrance and the slow but sure thrust as he entered her body for the first time brought tears of joy to her eyes.

"Jeran, will you move?" Ashley groaned impatiently at her mate. The contrasting personalities couldn't be more diverse. She loved them both in different but by no means less ways. Jeran's laugh at her comment, and the ensuing forceful thrusts as he became caught up in his passion, washed over and satisfied her.

Jarod stroked her hair back from her face, and then kissed her with growing passion. It was as though he had to touch her when he was near her. Jeran's grip grew stronger as he thrust into her pussy rapidly, moaning his pleasure as he did so. Ashley loved the way his cock reached her special spot; Jarod's had done the same but she had been so caught up in sensation that it never registered at the time.

She knew her orgasm was imminent, and from the sound of Jeran's ragged breathing, his was too. He brought her up close to his body, and she knew what was coming next. The sinking of his teeth in the sensitive area threw her into one orgasm and then another as his mouth sucked strongly, not taking too much, but enough to satisfy both of them. His own shudders as his seed drenched her womb brought a growl of satisfaction from his lips.

Yes, thought Ashley, *I am a lucky woman.* She let her mates soothe and cleanse her till they were satisfied. Although Ashley knew that the cleansing was for her comfort, she found herself becoming aroused again. What did she mean again? She seemed to have been continually aroused since she first saw them both.

She had been the one to benefit from their ministrations so far. She wanted to take the chance to explore their bodies. And what bodies they were. A shiver of delight ran through her as she realised they now belonged exclusively to her.

Running her hand over Jarod's chest, she touched his small, male nipples, one after the other. She revelled in the glazed look of passion in his eyes. Turning to Jeran she repeated her movements, and was pleased to have the same reaction.

Taking Jarod's nipple into her mouth she licked and nibbled, then moved downwards to his hard cock. Taking his length into her mouth she licked around the head, lapping the pre-come as his body let her know how much he was enjoying her touch. She felt Jeran behind her, moving her till she was on her hands and knees in a position that pleased him. The touch of his rough tongue on her pussy felt unbelievable.

Jarod caught the sides of her head, showing her the speed he wanted her to move. Caught between the two of them, she forgot the place, the time, everything. All that mattered was her mates and pleasure.

Moaning in protest as Jarod pulled his weeping cock from her mouth, Ashley felt Jeran leave her and move away. Turning, she watched as he walked over to the altar and picked up a little bowl.

Jarod caught her chin in his hand, turning her back toward him. "Do you trust us not to hurt you?"

Ashley was startled. Of course she trusted them; she wouldn't be here otherwise. Then she caught sight of what was in the bowl.

Oil.

They wanted to fuck her at the same time. One in her pussy and one in her ass.

Taking a deep breath, Ashley knew she could deny them nothing. She had known that this moment would come, but had thought that they would give her a bit more time to get used to having both of them as lovers. But maybe it was best to get the unknown over with as soon as possible.

"How -- how do you want me?"

As she watched the deep breaths both took, she realised they hadn't been sure she would allow this. She'd made the right choice.

Jarod moved to lie down. "Come here, Ashley."

She moved over his prone figure, kissing him as he ran his hands up and down her body, shifting her hips till her wet pussy was over his cock. "Take me inside you," whispered Jarod.

Lifting herself up, she lowered herself down on Jarod's hard length, moaning as her tissues were stretched. Jeran stroked her back, and then tilted her forwards till he had her in the right position. She felt warm, sticky fingers caressing her anus, teasing her. Then the slight pressure as he inserted one finger into the elastic sheath, moving back and forwards till she grew accustomed to the strange feeling of having something in her ass.

One finger gradually became two, then three. Ashley moaned as she started to enjoy the dual sensations of Jarod filling her pussy, and Jeran's fingers in her at the same time. She moaned as he withdrew from her ass, then felt the thick, blunt head of his oil-covered cock at her entrance. Tensing,

Ashley felt him stay still till she relaxed again, getting used to the pressure of him at her entrance. "It's all right, Jeran; you can move now."

As she finished speaking, he gave a quick squeeze of her hips, then the gentle push and withdrawal of his cock as he attempted to enter her. Then with a snap the elastic ring of her anus opened enough for the head of his cock to enter her ass. Ashley caught her breath at the invasion, but gradually became used to it, and moved her hips for Jeran to continue till at last his thick length filled her completely.

Ashley felt full. She was stuffed front and back and she loved it. Her mates began a gentle push and retreat. One would push, the other withdraw until she was overwhelmed by the sensations running through her body. They played her like an instrument, their groans of pleasure arousing her further. That she could give them this amount of satisfaction was overpowering to her.

She felt her orgasm flow through her body; her mates growled as her pussy and anus clenched and squeezed their cocks. Her body shuddered as the pleasure took over. The warm gush of seed in her pussy and the flow down her legs told her that Jarod and Jeran had succumbed to their own pleasure.

Yes, she was indeed a lucky woman.

Epilogue

Dressed once more in her lovely tunic, Ashley sat between Jeran and Jarod talking to Leah and Darius. Ashley was feeling overwhelmed by her actions in front of the crowd of Leopai and Jageri, but more so because Leah had been there to witness her behaviour.

Giving Leah a quick glance out of the corner of her eye, Ashley noticed she was grinning at her. "What are you smirking at?"

"You. I haven't seen you this quiet since the time you had that crush on…"

"Lee! I am just trying to get around the fact you saw me stark naked and making love. It's not exactly normal practice, you know. It will take me time to come to terms with that."

"It's normal for us, my mate. We are a race of strong sensuality, and we don't think there is anything wrong with mates pleasuring each other. Even in public places," Jeran whispered in her ear.

What she would have said in response to that she didn't know because there was a shout from the lookout tower in the compound. The men looked up to the sky to the north. Ashley followed their gaze and saw a bright, gleaming ship approach in the sky.

She turned toward her friend. "That is not one of ours, Lee." Turning toward Jarod she asked her mate, "Whose ship is that?"

At the same time she heard Leah say to Darius, "I didn't think you had this type of technology."

"I did say that we lived as we do out of choice, not necessity, my mate," Darius said, running a hand of comfort down Leah's arm.

Jarod turned to Darius, and inquired, "Who is at the City this term?"

"The Lioni," Jeran answered him before Darius could. "It is Garrick flying the ship and you know that he wouldn't be if it wasn't serious."

Ashley glanced from her mates to Leah and back, knowing that the same thoughts were running through Leah's mind. If they had ships, then why did they live such a basic lifestyle?

"We prefer to live life as free as we can, Ashley. We are in tune with nature and our surroundings. But that is not to say that we don't have technological skills we can call upon, too," said Jeran, answering her mental questions.

"Darius, what is this City you mentioned?" Leah asked the next question Ashley wanted an answer to.

"We -- all the packs -- take turns in monitoring and preserving the central place of our ancestors. We call it the City, as it was where we all lived at one time. We had just handed over caretaker-ship to the Lioni and had returned here, a few days before you crashed."

"Um, does that mean when we go the next time I can fly that ship?"

"Yes, Leah, if you so desire, you can fly the ship once I am confident you are familiar with the controls," Darius said with a sigh.

"What kind of fuel does it use? There are no fumes that I can see." Ashley was intrigued by the way the small ship handled and the lack of emissions coming from it.

"It is run by solar energy. We never use any fossil or other toxic fuel sources. We want to preserve our planet, not destroy it by burning chemical fuels," Jarod answered her question as he stood up with the other men, watching the little ship land outside the compound.

"Stay here. We will return soon."

Ashley looked at Leah; both watched their mates stride away with their men following them. Neither were the type of *stay there little woman* and their mates were going to find that out -- now.

As they stood up, Mata and Jilla joined them, shaking their heads. "Will we join the men?" Jilla asked. "I think this is something that concerns us all."

Ashley linked her arm with Leah and the four of them followed behind the retreating males. As they drew nearer the ship, she could see the smooth lines and compact design; it would be a joy to fly in.

Pushing through the group of men who parted for their Alpha females, Ashley saw a large male figure talking with her mates. And she meant large! If she thought Jarod and Jeran were tall and well built, this man was as close to seven feet as he could get. Waist length blond hair that he had tied back with a cord, high cheekbones and startling golden brown eyes were all that she had time to take in as her mates turned as one to look at her furiously as they picked up her thoughts.

"Ah, your mates have joined us, I see. Well, this does concern them both," the stranger declared. "I am pleased that my friends have found their mates. Welcome to Catari. I am here with news that will not please your mates, but there was no choice in my actions."

He took a deep breath before continuing, "There is a ship just outside the planet's orbit. It has been sitting there for the last day taking readings, and soon it will be able to scan this area."

"Is it one of ours looking for us? I knew they would come here," said Leah, turning into Darius's embrace.

"Don't worry, my mate, they will find nothing with their instruments," Darius murmured, running his hand over Leah's head.

"That is no longer an option, I am afraid, Darius. I apologise to you and to you both," he said, turning toward Jeran and Jarod. "I have taken down the force field you placed over the crashed shuttle your mates arrived on."

"What? Why would you do such a thing?" Jarod growled.

"Force field? You have force fields too?" Ashley was stunned at the information they were getting. At no time since she woke up did she think they had this much technology at their disposal.

"My own mate is on the rescue craft. It must be allowed to land on the planet."

Ashley watched as the angry expressions on her mates' faces turned to understanding. There would be a confrontation that none of them had expected, but they would prevail. Nothing else would be acceptable… for any of them.

Jilla listened as Garrick informed her Alpha and Shaman of the imminent arrival of the Skylian search party. What she hadn't wanted to admit to herself before now was that her own mate was one of the Skylians. She had been prepared to forgo him because she would never compromise her Alpha's happiness, but this put a different spin on the situation.

She now had a chance at happiness, of having young herself, something she had believed would never be possible, especially when her dream searching had taken her so far away. With the arrival of Ashley and Leah she was able to put the jigsaw of dreams together, but she knew it would be impossible to allow them to find the two females.

Now, if only her mate was not the man who had been promised to Ashley, she could have the life she wanted. But if it was the one who Ashley called Keevan, she saw no chance of mating with him and remaining with the Jageri. Jarod especially would never allow that to happen. He would not want to give Ashley constant reminders of her past life, not with someone who had obviously meant something to her.

Jilla felt Garrick's gaze. He knew somehow that her mate was also on that search craft. Shivering, she thought of the whispered power he was said to have. Like Jeran, he kept his abilities hidden. Unlike Jeran, she didn't know him.

Catari Heat 3: Mate Fever

Kyla Logan

Chapter One

"Asshole," whispered Kira under her breath as Jason moved through the doorway of the shuttle. Unfortunately it mustn't have been quiet enough as he turned back to face her with a furious expression.

Striding back toward her, he ground out angrily, "What did you say to me?"

Kira had put up with a lot from him and she was not going to put up with *his lordship* any longer; enough was bloody well enough. "You heard. Maybe you weren't supposed to, but you did, and I'll be glad to repeat it for you if you want."

She just about burst out laughing watching his face grow redder at her comments. Well, he was an asshole; pity he was adept at keeping this side of his personality hidden from the *powers that be* on the base ship, otherwise he would have been disciplined well before now. Kira really felt sorry for Leah -- having to mate with this guy.

"How dare you --"

Thankfully Kira didn't have to listen to another spiel from his ass-ship as Keevan, the ranking officer of this rescue mission, walked through the door, stopping Jason's rant.

"What's going on, people? We are on a rescue mission here; I need you all at your posts double-checking that your equipment is loaded and ready to go. We are just about to come out of leeway."

"Hi Keevan, just a difference of opinion, that's all," said Kira. Keevan was one of the few higher ranking men who actually realised what Jason was like.

"This bitch called me an asshole. I want her disciplined," Jason said angrily.

Kira watched Keevan's left eye twitch, a sure sign of his growing temper. She supposed she should feel sorry for Jason. Yeah… right!

"I hope I misheard you, Captain, because it sounds like I have grounds to put you on discipline for calling the doctor a bitch." Keevan stared down at the smaller man.

"I -- yes, Major, you misheard my comment." Red-faced with anger, Jason stood to attention.

"In that case go and do what I ordered; check your equipment," said Keevan, turning away and dismissing him.

Waiting till Jason had left the cabin, Keevan turned to Kira. "Can't you stay out of trouble? I know you don't like him, but we don't need things like this happening. Are your equipment and medical supplies ready for the landing?"

"Sorry Keev, he just frustrates me with his arrogant attitude. How on Skyla can you stand to have him as your second-in-command? You know he'll attempt to undermine you."

"There is no chance of that happening, not with everyone on board aware of what a bastard he is. But please, Kira, stay out of his way."

"He knows the minute I see Leah I'm going to tell her he tried to come on to me. You know that's his problem with me. I turned him down. Creep!"

Kira shuddered, wondering if his cousin was anything like him. Skyla! She hoped not or she would refuse to mate with him when he arrived at the next exchange of personnel.

Keevan would stand by her. She knew he wouldn't let her join with someone she didn't like.

"Major, we are leaving leeway and approaching the planet," announced the mission pilot over the communication system.

Keevan tapped the *com* pad on the back of his hand. "Stay out of orbit for the moment. I'll be right there." Turning toward the door he said to Kira, "After you have your medical supplies checked come to the bridge for debriefing."

"Yes, sir," Kira said softly as her brother strode out the door. She knew he was anxious to get the mission underway, but he would take no unnecessary risks. He would run a complete planet scan before taking up orbit. She wanted to be there when his ass-ship discovered they wouldn't be landing until Keevan was satisfied whatever happened to Ashley and Leah wouldn't happen to them.

* * *

Keevan studied the data from the planetary scans they had taken over the last day. Nothing! No sign of the shuttle. How on Skyla were their scans missing it? It had to be there -- somewhere.

"How long are we going to sit here? We have to get down on the planet and search."

Keevan turned to face a furious Jason. He was getting as tired of the bastard and his know-it-all attitude as everyone else. Even knowing what his insubordination could bring to him didn't seem to bother Jason in his dealings with the crew. But until he was given grounds for disciplining him -- strong grounds -- Keevan would just have to bite his tongue and put up with him.

"Do you have the coordinates of the exact location the shuttle landed? If you do then give them to me and we'll land near it. Otherwise get back to your post and get the readings we are all looking for."

Hearing a chuckle from the doorway, Keevan looked away from the source of his annoyance and watched his sister enter the flight deck. The snarl from Jason brought Keevan's attention firmly back to the problem at hand.

"We need to find them, and we can't sitting here. At least let us take up an orbiting position…"

Keevan cut off that line of complaint right away. "We were ordered to take extensive readings before moving into orbit, Captain. You were there at the same briefing as everyone else on this ship. Until we have details of where the shuttle landed, we are not moving one inch closer to that planet. Do I make myself clear?"

"Yes sir, you make yourself very clear," grunted Jason as he turned back to his instrument panel.

"Glad that's sorted out. We'll run another complete sweep of the planet, everyone. There has to be some sign of the shuttle; we just have to keep looking." Keevan turned toward Kira as she moved closer.

"You need a break, Major. You have been awake long past the end of your duty shift."

Keevan knew she was right, but he had a feeling that he was going to be needed on the bridge. He didn't want to leave right now. "Give me a stimulant. I need to be here now." Seeing the frown on her face, he drew her to one side away from the rest of the bridge crew. "I don't trust a certain captain to follow orders, Kira. I need to stay awake. At least until he is off duty and Xavier is here to relieve me."

Comprehension flashed over Kira's face. "Do you have five minutes to spare so you can at least eat something while I get a hypo?"

"That should work. Sorry to put you in this position, but..."

"I understand, Keev. Go have a hot drink and I'll bring you something to help you keep going." Kira turned away and headed for the door.

Breathing a sigh of relief, Keevan walked over to the pilot and whispered that he would be back in fifteen minutes.

Just as he reached the door an astonished Thera exclaimed, "What on Skyla?" Turning round he was surprised when she brought up readings of the shuttle on the main screen.

"The shuttle was *not* there a few seconds ago, Major. It just *appeared*."

"Show me the previous recordings, Thera," Keevan said, then stopped when Jason broke in.

"How could it just appear? You are trying to cover up for not seeing it before!"

"That is enough, Captain. I don't want another word out of you. In fact, you are now officially off duty, and I want you off my bridge," Keevan said softly.

Turning back to Thera, he squeezed her shoulder to let her know he knew she hadn't missed seeing the shuttle. He was rewarded by a hesitant smile of relief.

"I'm not leaving when..."

Keevan felt a growing headache pierce his skull at Jason's words. He didn't even turn to look at him to give him a response. If he had he would have decked him, he was so angry. "Security, escort the captain to his quarters. He is off duty until I say otherwise."

He tried to ignore the muffled curses thrown his way as Jason was escorted off the bridge. But the relieved sighs from the remaining Skylians told him he had made the right decision.

"Thera, contact Blue team and ask them to resume their duty shift. I think we all need to take a break, and let fresh eyes work out exactly how the shuttle's readings appeared so suddenly."

At least his report would show that everyone on this particular shift went off duty just after the removal of Jason. How his actions would be perceived by the *powers that be* would be another thing entirely.

Chapter Two

Jilla woke up with a start. She'd been dreaming of her mate again, but this time she remembered more of his features. He had light-coloured green eyes and close-cropped blond hair; his face was much leaner than the males of the Jageri clan -- in fact of any of the packs of Catari.

She had known for a while that her chosen was not a male of Catari. He wasn't all that much taller than she was, maybe five foot ten or eleven, with a wiry build. Not overly muscular, as the Jageri males were, but she could see he kept himself fit.

Jilla sighed. Knowing he was of a different race didn't worry her so much, not when they would be joined at the mating ceremony.

Yesterday, seeing how happy her Alpha and Shaman were at finally mating with Ashley had been heartwarming. They had both been so worried about her head injury. But that was in the past; she had to look to her future now. All she could do was be patient until the fates brought her mate into her life. And after the news that Garrick of the Lioni brought, she knew that she didn't have long to wait.

He was a member of the Skylians' search party, so there was a good chance that he had been the intended mate of Leah or Ashley. How would Jarod and Jeran feel if her mate turned out to be one of these males? Well, for pack unity she just hoped it was someone not connected intimately to the two females.

But for now she could remember the touch of her own mate. Yes, it was only in her dreams, but that was all she had to comfort herself with until she met him face to face.

* * *

His beautiful eyes sparkled in delight when he saw her waiting for him again. The touch of his lips against hers made her pussy weep in anticipation of being filled with his cock.

Being the same height brought a new thrill to her; she could feel his growing hardness where it belonged… pressing against her pussy.

She took the initiative and unzipped his tunic, loving the look of his muscular torso when it was revealed. He was hairier than the Jageri males, but she found that she liked the texture as she ran her fingers through his chest hair before finding the little nubbin of his nipple.

Bending slightly she took one hard point in her mouth; his sigh of enjoyment encouraged her to lick and nibble her way from one to the other.

His hands clasped her head, and his fingers massaged her scalp in time to her sucking. Then he pulled her away and brought her nearer to accept his kiss. His marauding tongue demanded a response from her.

She felt his hands move to unfasten her tunic straps, then the tug to remove it from her torso, to slide it down over her hips. Nothing stood in his way of exploring her body now.

Breaking free from his kiss, she felt the pinch of his fingers on her nipples. Jilla closed her eyes, enjoying the pleasure/pain of his touch. He kissed her jaw and neck then licked one erect nipple. Drawing the tip in his mouth, he sucked strongly on it. A flush of moisture flowed from her pussy at the delicious sensations his touch brought to her.

"Please, I need more," Jilla moaned as she pushed his tunic down over his shoulders and arms. She felt impatient for his total possession this time.

Shrugging off his clothes, he dropped down to his knees in front of her and gently moved her legs apart so that he was able to see her pussy. Jilla ran her fingers over his hair, and pushed him closer. She could feel her juices running down the inside of her legs and knew he had to see how needy she was for the touch of his mouth.

She gave a sigh of pleasure at the first swipe of his wet tongue as he licked the trail of moisture back to the place it flowed from. She purred as he licked from clit to anus and back, then took the little bundle of nerves into his mouth and sucked. The loving touch of her mate brought her to orgasm so quickly.

Her heart overflowed with a feeling of happiness as she looked down into his eyes. He would never let her go; she knew that from his expression.

Breaking free from her gaze he once more lapped at her pussy, pushing his tongue as far as it would go inside her, alternately flattening, and then rolling it, providing her with a multitude of sensations that threatened to bring her to her knees.

Drawing away from her pussy with obvious regret, he pulled her down in front of him. As he kissed her, she tasted herself mingled with his own unique taste. It was a powerful combination that she discovered she enjoyed very much.

"I need you inside me, now," said Jilla, breathless from his kiss. She saw the glazed look in his eyes at her words and knew that he felt the same.

Jilla lay on the ground and pulled him toward her, felt the hard, thick length of his cock against her leg as he moved into position above her. Then the damp tip pressing against her opening.

Looking down she saw one inch then another slowly enter her pussy; the sensation of fullness caused her to close her eyes in delight. She let her head fall back as finally the last inch was inserted deep inside her.

"Look at me, baby. I want you to know who you belong to."

Her eyes flew open at his words. His slow movements were killing her. She needed him to move faster, but didn't want to spoil the moment in any way.

Thankfully he seemed to need the same thing as he began to speed up. The thrusts were deeper and varied as he shifted his hips to gain deeper penetration.

Bringing her legs up and around his waist, she gave him the chance to go farther than before. As she dug her nails into his shoulders to encourage his thrusts, the speed and his thickness threw her into a second orgasm, one that caught them both in its grasp. Her internal muscles clamped on his cock, sending him into his own release. Jilla felt the hot splash of his come and the shudders he made as he achieved his own satisfaction before finally collapsing on top of her.

Stroking his damp hair, she listened as the harshness of his breathing became calmer. She knew that their time was drawing to a close, but wanted to savour their lovemaking for a little while longer.

He raised his head from her breasts and looked down into her eyes. "This feels so real, not as dreamlike as it normally is. How can that be?" His body started to fade before her. She heard the masculine denial that fell from his lips and could have cried.

* * *

Jilla felt the wetness on her lashes, and would have given anything to be beside him now. She could swear she could smell his scent on her skin, the dream had felt so real. The stickiness between her legs even seemed too copious to come just from her own orgasm. Running her finger over her pussy lips she brought the moisture to her nose.

She did smell him… there were two distinct and separate scents. Flinging the cover away, Jilla noticed the little love bruise on her breast.

How was this possible?

Chapter Three

Keevan woke up from another amazing dream. This one had seemed so much clearer and more real than any of the others. He'd seen his beautiful lover for the first time without anything obscuring his vision. She had lovely topaz eyes and long, golden blonde hair that had swept down over her shoulders. She was only slightly shorter than him, and that was something he wasn't used to. As one of the tallest Skylians on the base ship he had gotten used to towering over the females -- apart from Kira -- and most of the men.

Shifting slightly he felt a sharp pain in his shoulders… and the wetness around his cock and belly. Skyla, these wet dreams had to stop. He was too old for them.

Getting up just as his intercom rang, he touched the *com* on his hand.

"Yes, what have you to report?"

"The survey is complete, Major. Should I wake Red team now?"

"Go ahead, Xavier. I'll have a quick shower and join everyone for the debriefing."

Moving to his shower cubicle, Keevan noticed that he could still smell his lover on his skin. Looking in the mirror he noticed that his back was covered with small scratches. He remembered her digging her nails into him while he thrust into her.

But how did he end up marked?

He had no time for confusing thoughts right now; this would have to wait till he had time to think. Entering the small cubicle he pressed the button and waited for the sonic waves to cleanse him of his dream encounter, wishing there was some way he could keep the scent of his lover a little longer, but that was impossible.

There was too much at stake to start thinking about a dream… even one that somehow left marks.

Dressed once more, Keevan left his room and strode toward the bridge, nodding to the members of his team as they joined him.

Entering the flight deck Keevan moved toward Xavier, the leader of Blue team and his life-long friend. He wouldn't have trusted anyone else on board to make sure the survey was completed without him nearby.

Skyla, was Jason still confined to his quarters? He had totally forgotten the bastard was there.

"I told them to let a certain pain-in-the-ass out, don't worry, Keevan," Xavier said quietly, noticing the expression on his face. The two of them always had an uncanny knack of knowing what the other was thinking… without using their telepathic gifts openly.

Laying a hand on his shoulder, Keevan said, "Thanks, friend. Now tell me what you have discovered."

"Want to wait for him?" asked Xavier.

"Nope, everyone else is here, so talk away." Keevan looked up as Kira and the two crewmen who had been dispatched to let Jason out of his room walked onto the flight deck.

"We did a complete comparison from before the shuttle *appeared* on the screen and just after. There are residual traces of delta waves surrounding the shuttle, which seems to hint at some sort of shield being used to mask it from our sensors. In-depth analysis shows that there was an increased quantity of delta waves on our previous scans of that area."

"So it looks like the natives have some kind of shielding technology at their disposal," Keevan stated.

"Yep. The area surrounding the shuttle is forest, but about five klicks further in, there appears to be a native village of some sort. I'd say if we can't find the girls near the shuttle, we'll find them there." Xavier broke off whatever else he was going to say next as Jason made his appearance.

"How dare…"

Keevan felt his eye twitch at the start of what would probably be a long speech. He wasn't in the mood for it today.

"Sit down, and listen to the debriefing. If you have any complaints write it in your mission report. Carry on, Xavier."

Xavier's lips gave a twitch of a smile as some of the crew snorted in response to their commander's words.

"About fifty klicks further away from that compound is another one, similar to this one. But we have not managed to scan them as deeply as we would like to. Something is blocking us from that. I would say it's a device similar to the one used to hide the shuttle, but at a lower setting."

"All right, I think we have enough information to mount a reconnaissance mission with shuttle Alpha. Doctor, you'll be part of this crew in case Ashley and Leah need medical help. The rest of you know the drill. Be ready to go in fifteen minutes," Keevan said, then turned to Xavier. "Take up orbit, Captain, but be careful."

"Thera, take us into position above the crash site. Keep it steady." Xavier sat in the commander's chair watching carefully as the pilot made adjustments to her controls. The jolt that ran through the ship as orbit was stabilised drew a breath of relief from everyone.

"Well done, Thera. Xavier, walk with me to the shuttle." Keevan moved toward the door knowing that his friend would follow.

"Give your crew some downtime, Xavier, yourself included. Thera and the others staying from Red team will cope and they can *com* you if they need you for anything. I want Blue team rested in case I need them on the planet."

"Will do. I hope we are not needed, but we'll be ready if the call comes." Xavier stopped before the hangar bay door. "Watch your back down there; I don't want to lose a friend."

Keevan met Xavier's eyes, knowing what he was hinting at without words. It wasn't just the possibility of native troubles, but from one of their own.

"I'll be careful. Don't worry so much." Keevan clasped Xavier's arm in a warrior grasp, then moved toward the waiting shuttle.

Once inside he strapped himself into his seat, and let the pilot run last minute checks. Looking around at the ten-man crew, he saw that they were busy preparing themselves for departure. Kira winked at him when she caught his gaze. She was a damn fine doctor -- he just hoped she wouldn't be needed. "Alpha shuttle ready for departure, bridge."

"Opening the bay door now. Good fortune, everyone," Thera's voice came over the *com*.

Keevan felt the shuttle lift off the floor of the hangar, moving slowly at first, then with increasing speed as it left the ship behind. Knowing it would take some time to reach their comrades' fallen craft, he began to study the readings Xavier's team had taken -- planning the best route toward the settlement that had been spotted.

Chapter Four

Garrick, Alpha of the Lioni pack of Catari, closed his eyes as he listened to his brother's voice.

"The ship took up orbit a short time ago, Garrick. And a minute ago they launched a shuttle," Ranen said.

"They are heading toward the crashed shuttle?" Garrick asked the question, already knowing the answer.

"Yes. Is she on board, Garrick?" Ranen asked in a hesitant voice.

"I can sense her coming closer, so yes, she must be on board this ship. Keep us informed of any further developments, Ranen. I'll talk with you later." Garrick switched off the radio and turned to face the three men beside him.

Jarod, Alpha of the Jageri, turned toward his brother Jeran. "We know where our pack is to take position; I'll go and lead them. I want you to stay with Ashley."

Jeran looked deeply into his brother's eyes, and then said, "Very well. I feel better knowing one of us is protecting her anyway. Although I would have liked to help with these strangers who think they can take our mate from us."

Turning to face Darius, Alpha of the Leopai, in whose territory this confrontation would occur, Jeran said, "I'll of course put Leah under my protection while you are seeing to these men."

His lips twitching, Darius replied, "I never thought the day would come when I would leave my mate's well-being in the hands of a Jageri Shaman. My thanks, Jeran. I know you'll care for both our mates while we take care of any trouble."

Garrick stood up, eager to join in the hunt with the Jageri and Leopai packs. He had a mate to claim.

The four men left the control room that housed the radio, and met four completely different women in the passageway.

Leah and Ashley were more alike than the other two, both petite in build but with different personalities. The other two women were native Catarian, and towered over Leah and Ashley. Jilla, the Jageri Seer, with her long, golden blonde hair was a contrast to Mata, the Leopai Seer, who had equally long, but dark hair.

All four had serious expressions on their faces.

Leah was the first to speak. "You have to promise that no one will be hurt, Darius, on either side. Please, this is important to me. Both Ashley and I have been talking. We need to make them understand that we are happy here and would never leave our mates."

"You are staying in the compound, Leah. No more discussion on this. I need to know you are safe," Darius growled.

"But..." Ashley was cut off by Jeran.

"I'm staying with the two of you, while the others deal with this situation. You will both be under my protection," Jeran stated.

Leah and Ashley argued with their mates every time Garrick saw them together. They wouldn't win this argument, but it was fun to see the other Alphas having problems controlling them.

He would never let his mate argue with him in public.

Looking over at the blonde-haired Seer, he waited for her contribution to this argument. It was about time she told them that her own mate was on the craft coming toward them. Oh, he understood the reasons behind her reluctance to tell her Alpha and Shaman, but she was running out of time.

Jilla cleared her throat, catching the others' attention. "I'm going with you all."

"No."

"It's too risky."

Jilla held up her hand to stop Jarod and Jeran from saying more.

"I haven't told you everything. I didn't know how to." Breaking off, she glanced at Leah and Ashley, then back to the males. "My own mate is on the shuttle. I don't know who but I'll know him by sight from my dreams."

Pandemonium broke out, everyone trying to talk at once, with questions flung in Jilla's direction. Garrick knew he had better step in or they would never leave the Pantheri compound.

"Now that is out of the way, we can get moving. The ship is getting closer all the time, and we need to join our men and get in position. Jilla has the right to claim her mate as much as I do this day." Turning toward her, he said, "Keep close to me as much as you can. For some reason I think our mates will be together."

Ashley gave a gasp, which caught all their attention.

"Is there something we should know, Ashley?" Jarod asked.

After a quick glance at Leah, who nodded her head, Ashley said, "Just when you said that they might be together, I'm wondering if it might be Keevan and Kira. They are brother and sister, although Kira has never been on a mission like this one before. Being a doctor she might have been included because of Keevan."

"I recognise that name. He was to be your Skylian mate!" Jarod growled.

Jilla closed her eyes, pain written all over her face at hearing the conversation.

Ashley moved close and put a hand on her arm. "If Keevan is your mate you couldn't have a more caring man."

She stopped on hearing the growls coming from Jeran's and Jarod's throats. Turning toward them she put her hands on her hips.

"Give it a rest; he has always been like a big brother to me, even though we were to be mates. I can't think of a better mate for Jilla than him."

Jarod stopped growling with a struggle. "Seer, we'll discuss this later. Our main concern is to neutralise any threats. We can talk about your mate when we are all safe." He turned away and walked to the exit. Garrick followed.

* * *

Kira stepped off the shuttle into the blindingly hot and humid day. The heat was overpowering. Sweat ran down her back under the flight suit she had on. She unzipped her tunic, noticing that everyone was doing the same. Taking it off helped a bit; at least the short-sleeved vest was cooler.

Looking around she noticed the damaged shuttle that Leah had been piloting. What a mess! She hoped the two women had escaped any serious injury. And if not, that's what she was here for, once they found them.

She turned back when she heard Keevan say, "We will form two teams; you know already who your leader is. Team two, I want you to explore the shuttle, find out as much as you can, then join the rest of us looking for signs of Leah and Ashley."

Putting on her backpack with her medical supplies, she moved to Keevan's side. She noticed the disgruntled looks of everyone that was on Jason's team. But there was nothing she could do to help them out; she just had to be prepared for anything.

"I don't think they'll find much, so let's see what we find in the area surrounding the shuttle. Stay close, Kira."

Kira shook her head; big brothers could be too overprotective.

A shout from inside the craft halted their immediate search. Keevan moved nearer to the entrance to find out what had caused such a reaction.

"Someone tried to fix the communication station, but they didn't have much success." Jason paused. "One of them was hurt, how badly we can't tell, but it looks like they tried to splint up either an arm or leg."

Kira frowned. "Why didn't they just use the mediKit?"

"Maybe because it's been smashed to bits?" Jason sneered at her.

"All right, that's enough. Keep searching to see if you come up with any more clues." Turning away toward his own team, he said, "Have you found anything yet?"

"Yes, Major, it looks like there was a pack of animals around this area, then there are men's footprints."

"Let me see," Keevan said, moving toward Soren. "Yes, they headed in that direction, further into the forest -- heading toward the settlement we saw on our scans."

Tapping his *com* pad on his hand, Keevan said, "Team two, we are heading out in the direction of the built up area. Follow us when you finish your search."

"Will do, Major."

More affirmatives came over the *com*. Keevan turned to her and said, "Let's go, Kira. Stay close, there is no telling when or if we'll run into the animals that made these tracks.

They look like big brutes and I don't want you on your own."

Kira sighed. "Keev, I'm an adult. It's not like I go looking for trouble."

Shaking his head, he started walking toward the rest of the team who waited at the entrance to the forest area. Kira was looking forward to this part; there was no telling what plants were growing in such a humid area. Hopefully she would find time to take some samples for the botanists... and for herself.

Kira wiped the sweat off her brow. Stopping, she took her water bottle out of her backpack and took a long cool drink, recapped it and put it away again. Retying her hair in a ponytail, she took a good look around. The different shades of green of the trees and plants complemented the flowers of red and orange that grew in and around them. There were beautiful specimens that she knew the botanists on her base ship would love to study in more depth. Taking some sample jars from her pack, she clipped some plants carefully and stored them in her sample case. Once she started she lost track of time, only noticing that she was alone when the forest around her grew deadly quiet.

Looking quickly around, she saw there was no sign of the rest of her team. "*Skyla,* Keevan was right. I need a keeper."

Before she could hit her *com* on her hand, there was a rustle of plants, then they parted as the head of one of the largest animals she had ever seen pushed its way through.

Kira sagged back against the trunk on the tree nearest her. Watching as the massive beast emerged from his hiding place, she couldn't help but admire the beauty of the animal. As the cat drew nearer, Kira found it was hard to keep calm. It was about ten feet in length and at least four hundred pounds, with a lithe and muscular body. The rounded head had prominent whiskers and the glorious mane that surrounded his head, neck, and even his undersides, was a rich golden brown.

"Why on Skyla am I paying so much attention to its looks? I should be climbing the nearest tree."

But it was hard not to be impressed by the savage beauty of the beast. She was startled by its actions. Instead of leaping on her as she thought it would, he lay down, stretching as far as he could, keeping hold of her gaze with his warm golden brown eyes. Kira held her breath, waiting for his next move. What he did next surprised her even more; he crawled along the forest floor, inching nearer and nearer.

Mouth open in surprise, Kira let herself slide down the tree she was leaning on, until she sat on the ground. The cat waited till she was still again then continued his slow and careful crawl until his massive head slightly touched her legs. When she didn't retreat from his light touch, he moved closer until he could rest his head completely on her outstretched legs, looking into her eyes the entire time.

Taking a shuddering breath, Kira lifted a shaking hand and slowly stroked the top of his large head. When the cat's eyes closed and a deep purr came from his throat, she grew bolder in her caress. She had never been in a situation like this. That a wild animal would let her touch him instead of biting off her hand was unbelievable. But she was also getting a tickling sensation in her head, one similar but not exactly the same as when she linked telepathically with her brother.

It was as though a voice was telling her not to fear this large cat, but to trust him with her life.

The butt of his head against her hand told her that she had stopped stroking him, something that he wasn't happy about by the absence of purring. She ran her fingers through his thick mane again, and the purrs grew louder than before.

"Well, I think I can safely say that you are not going to attack me, Mr. Cat. But why are you acting this way around me?" Kira kept her voice low and soothing. The cat opened his eyes at her words and shook his head, dislodging her hand. He gave her palm a little lick, as though in thanks for the rub then stood up and bounded back into the forest.

Kira was disappointed that her encounter had finished so abruptly. Standing up, she picked up and put on her backpack, and just as she was going to *com* Keevan, a rustling came from behind her. Turning swiftly, she saw the largest man she had ever seen come out from behind some bushes.

He had to be at least six foot nine or more. His long blond hair was tied back, and when his golden brown eyes met hers she forgot how to breathe.

Chapter Five

Garrick thought his initial encounter with his mate in cat form went very well. She had accepted his presence with surprisingly little fear. Now to introduce her to the man.

Masking her disappearance from the rest of the Skylians had been easy for him. He hoped when he let the illusion drop that Jilla would take the chance to finally meet her own mate.

But for now all he was concerned about was his mate.

Holding out a hand, Garrick said, "I won't hurt you, little one. I was just curious about you."

"I -- it's all right, you just startled me a little. I didn't think there was anyone nearby."

Garrick felt his cock harden at the sound of her voice. It was a soft sultry tone that went well with her beautiful features. She was taller than the two other Skylian women, maybe about five feet six inches. Her ash blonde hair was tied up in a ponytail. He looked forward to seeing it caress her face and neck when loose.

Her light green eyes had been busy cataloguing his features as he was hers. Meeting her gaze, he saw the humour shining back at him as both caught the other staring. "My name is Garrick. What's yours? I can't keep calling you little one."

She kept on surprising him, as she stepped forward with a grin and held out her hand to him. "My name is Kira. I'm the doctor with the search party that is looking for our two friends. Maybe you know where they were taken?"

The last was said hesitantly as he grasped her small hand in his. Garrick closed his eyes at the touch of his mate. He could see now why mates were claimed immediately.

"Are you all right? You look flushed and in pain. I have something that would help. Let me get my mediKit."

She broke off as he pulled her closer toward him. He couldn't resist taking her in his arms and inhaling her scent. Pure woman mixed with vanilla, not that he expected anything different. She was his mate.

Garrick took advantage of her surprise to bend down and give her neck a little lick. Her taste rushed through his body right to his groin. His cock grew harder and thicker, and his balls drew up tightly.

Releasing his grip, he stepped back slightly and watched her expression at his actions. He noticed the glazed look in her eyes. Her body recognised him, even if her brain hadn't caught on yet. Her nipples were tight little buds that showed through her vest top. He was hard pressed not to give in to his inclinations of taking one into his mouth. But he was trying to go as slow as he could.

Reaching out and taking hold of the hand that had her communication pad on it, he stroked his finger over the top, using his mental powers to disrupt the components. Once he was sure the link was severed, he touched the mind of Jilla.

I am dropping the illusion of my mate being with her group, Seer. Good hunting.

Garrick didn't wait for a response. He took back his power into himself, instantly feeling recharged and better able to cope with the side effects of being with his unclaimed mate.

"Why did you do that? Is that the way your people greet strangers?" Kira asked, shakily touching her neck.

Garrick noticed her eyes clearing as she waited for his response. He could lie to her, but that was not how he wanted to start their relationship.

"No, little one, it's the way I welcome my mate, now that I have finally met her."

Kira swallowed before saying, "Mate? What do you mean mate?"

"I know this is a surprise..."

"You're telling me!"

"But I can explain," Garrick carried on as though she hadn't interrupted him. "If we had more time and the circumstances were different, I would let you have longer to become acquainted with me before springing this on you. But we don't have time."

Kira nibbled her bottom lip as she studied his face, taking in what he had said to her. He felt a spurt of pre-come erupt from his stone hard cock. Garrick wanted her lips wrapped around his organ instead of being mangled by her teeth.

"Your people expected us to search for Leah and Ashley, didn't they? I can see the names mean something to you. Are they both well?"

"They are both in good health, little mate, and eagerly awaiting your arrival."

"At the shuttle it looked as though one or both was injured."

"Yes, Ashley had a serious head injury, but her mates cured her with the help of a few others," said Garrick, taking advantage of her distraction at his answers to move closer to her until he was touching her once more.

"Mates? As in more than one?" sputtered Kira.

Grinning, Garrick said, "Yes, she has the Alpha and the Shaman of the Jageri pack as her mates. Leah also has a mate in Darius, Alpha of the Leopai. This is his land that we are on."

"But -- but Ashley was to be my brother's mate when they returned home. How could she join with someone else? *Skyla*, not just one but two!"

Putting his arm around her shoulder, Garrick removed her backpack and slung it over one shoulder. Then he drew her close to his side and steered her in the direction of the Leopai stronghold.

"When you meet them you'll see why both claimed her and how happy she is with them. Leah seems to be happy too."

"Oh, that's good to hear." Then with a wide grin, she said, "That is really, really great news about Leah. I can't wait to see the asshole's face when he realises that Leah won't be joining with him."

"Asshole?"

"Oh, sorry. If Keevan heard me! I call Leah's former mate-to-be that because he is!" Kira said defiantly.

Garrick chuckled at her mutinous expression. "I'm sure he is, Kira." Dropping his arm from her shoulders, he moved slightly in front to clear a path through a particularly overgrown area. If he had been in his cat form the high tangles wouldn't have bothered him, but they needed to be cleared away to walk through in human form.

Kira followed the large male in front of her. She could hardly comprehend what he'd told her. Both Leah and Ashley… mated with natives of this planet. It was unbelievable, but for some reason she knew Garrick spoke truthfully. She stopped. How was she so sure she could trust what he said? She didn't know him.

"Don't fall behind, Kira. You could easily get lost in this forest."

Looking up, she couldn't help but notice the rippling muscles of Garrick's back and arms as he cleared the path for them. Wow, he was a delicious piece of eye candy. The very minimalist clothing he had on left nothing, and she meant nothing, to the imagination. In fact it only made her mouth water at the thought of what it did hide from her sight. When he had her in his arms she had *felt* the hard bulge, but would love to see it. Skyla, she was a letch!

Giggling under her breath, she followed Garrick once more, admiring the clenching and unclenching of his buttocks as he walked in front of her.

Garrick looked over his shoulder. "What is so funny?"

She noticed the flushed look on his face again. Thank Skyla he didn't know her latest thoughts; he would be more than flushed if he had.

"Oh, just that when I got up today I didn't think I would be trekking through a forest with one of the planet's indigenous people. You have to admit that is pretty amusing. Especially if you have talked to either of the women, then you would know how this sort of thing is not encouraged by the *powers that be* of our people. I just find it funny."

Garrick moved on once more, but said, "I had heard from Darius how insular your society is. He mentioned that Leah is the daughter of your commander."

Kira swallowed and moved her eyes off his bottom reluctantly, though anywhere she looked she felt her mouth growing dry. There had to be something that would take her mind off the gorgeous man in front of her.

"Kira?"

"Oh, um yes. That's right, it's one of the reasons I'm along. He was worried she would need urgent medical attention."

"Well, I'm glad you are here, whatever your reason for being part of your search party. Tell me something, my mate, the way you talked of this Jason. Is he going to be a problem for Leah?"

"Yes. If there is a way to warn Leah and Darius, well then I think you better do so." Kira wondered where her brain was. She should have contacted Keevan to let him know she was all right. He would be frantic. But why hadn't he tried to *com* her himself?

Stopping, she tapped the back of her hand, and said, "Keevan, this is Kira." She waited a few seconds and tried again with a frown. "Keevan?"

Looking up as Garrick returned to her side, she said, "My *com* doesn't seem to be working. No wonder I haven't had a lecture from my brother about getting separated from the group."

Garrick cupped her chin in his large hand, thumb caressing her cheek. "You are safe, and so are the rest of your people. You'll all be reunited at the Leopai stronghold." He dropped his hand and once more started to clear a path for them both.

"And I'm just supposed to believe that you know everyone is safe?"

"What does your heart tell you, Kira?"

It was a good question. Ever since his first touch she had been drawn to him. It wasn't just that he was gorgeous. That was only a lovely side benefit. For some reason she knew she could trust him with her life. And that had never happened to her before. This was something to really think about.

She was so lost in thought she wasn't aware of Garrick stopping until she walked into his back. He moved fast, turning round and steadying her.

Looking way up, she noticed the amused look in his eyes. She didn't take offence; she had been daydreaming. Being so close to him again, she noticed the delicious scent of musky male with -- what was that? Vanilla? She hadn't expected that particular fragrance on a man, but it was essentially *Garrick*.

"I thought you might like the opportunity to freshen up. There's a small waterfall and a pool this way," Garrick said before loosening his hold on her.

"Oh, that would be great, Garrick. Thank you for thinking of it."

A big smile covered his face as he drew her in the direction of the sound she was now aware of. Walking beside Garrick into the lovely opening, she took in the little waterfall and pool. It looked just big enough to immerse herself in.

Kira quickened her footsteps, eager to splash some cold water over her hot face. Garrick followed her, placing her backpack down and joining her in splashing his face with the cool liquid.

"It's safe to drink," Garrick said then cupped his hands and offered her some water.

All the warnings about not taking any of the local water or food until it had been tested went completely out of her head. Kira bent and drank the water Garrick offered her.

Her body reacted to his nearness, to the personal side of taking liquid from his hands. Her nipples hardened so much she felt them poking out from under her vest. She knew the exact moment Garrick saw her reaction to him. She heard his indrawn breath before he ran his damp hands under her hair and clasped her neck, gently pulling her closer toward him.

"I tried to go slowly, my mate, but I have to touch you," growled Garrick.

Sparks seemed to ignite when his lips met hers. Kira opened her mouth and let his marauding tongue take control. Running her hands over his arms and then around his back, she felt the massive muscles that she had been admiring such a short time ago.

Breaking free of his kiss so she could breathe, Kira noticed that she was the right height to lick his nipples. The tight puckered buds just cried out for her mouth.

The groan Garrick gave when she fastened her mouth over one nipple encouraged her to continue. He ran his hands over her breasts and down to the hem of her vest. Pulling it up, he caressed her sides then up toward her unfettered nipples. His thumbs and fingers pulled and squeezed in time to the sucks she gave his.

"Enough. Let me take this top off you, little mate," Garrick said huskily.

Kira was caught up in the moment. Her teachings against such actions went completely out of her mind. All she knew was that she had never felt such instant desire or trust for a Skylian that she had with Garrick... who was a stranger.

She helped him pull the vest over her head, saw it drop to the ground beside her backpack then felt Garrick's hands at the zip on her trousers. Wanting to get them off as quickly as possible, she pushed his hands aside, unzipped them and leaned on him as she stepped out of them.

The look on his face as he saw her naked form drew a blush from her. As a doctor she was used to the nude body, but for the first time in her life she was intimately aware of the differences between the male and female body.

Garrick dropped to his knees, leaned in and kissed her stomach. Kira's heart jumped in her chest at his actions. It was the tenderness she saw mixed with the desire in his face that caught her breath.

She was starting to believe his claim that she was his mate.

Garrick planted little kisses on her body as he made his way down. "Your pussy is smooth, just the way I like it," groaned Garrick.

Garrick moved her legs apart and licked her labial folds. Shivering with delight, Kira opened her legs wider to let him explore deeper. She was rewarded by a purring sound from deep in his throat.

Purring?

All thoughts left her as he inserted one finger into her pussy, using gentle in and out motions that along with his licking tongue banished any type of rational thinking.

As Garrick licked her, Kira took the opportunity to see what his marvellous, waist long hair looked like out of the cord he was using to tie it back. Moaning as Garrick replaced one finger with two, she pulled his hair closer and untied it. Running her hands through the thick tresses, she brought some to her face and sniffed the totally masculine scent that was *Garrick*. "Skyla, Garrick. You smell wonderful. I wish I could bottle it!"

A rumble of laughter came from his throat at her words. Taking his mouth off her pussy, he looked up into her eyes with his own passion-filled golden brown ones. "You don't need a bottle to remember my scent. You will be with me for the rest of our lives, Kira," said Garrick before he buried his face between her legs once more.

Pulling on his hair to get his attention, Kira blushed as she said, "I want to taste you."

He closed his eyes at her words, then withdrew his fingers from her depths, licked them and stood up again. "Where do you want me?"

Skyla, how to answer that? "Um, take off your -- what is this called anyway?" she said, tugging at his covering.

Grinning, he told her, "My loincloth?" And without waiting for her reply, he unfastened it and let it drop on the ground.

The sight that met her gaze made her draw in a deep breath. The veins running along the length of his long and thick cock were raised and prominent, the bulbous tip wet with moisture. Kira licked her lips then looked up at Garrick. He seemed to know why she was hesitant and said huskily, "Kneel down and lick me, please."

When she left her base ship she had never imagined she would be in this situation. But it all seemed to be so... right. She knelt down in front of his jutting cock and took it between her palms. It felt so soft and silky on the outside, but hard as stone in the centre. What did he taste like?

She ran her tongue over the tip and removed the white bead of pre-come. Groaning at the salty/musky taste, she licked her way down one side and back again. His purr startled her for a minute, but she ignored it and licked all around the top and into the little opening at the tip of his cock, eager for more.

She palmed his balls gently, knowing how sensitive they were, and moved down toward them. Taking the sac into her mouth, she tongued the two balls inside the sac, and then let them slip out once more.

His purring became louder.

Kira looked up at Garrick. The glazed look in his eyes took her breath away. He was magnificent. So tall, so broad and so muscled.

Were all the natives of this planet the same?

Garrick drew her up until she was standing in front of him. He didn't appear content with that and lifted her up into his arms, until she was face to face with him.

"If we carry on, I will claim you and never let you go, Kira. You have a choice to make. If we make love now before our mating ceremony, I won't come inside you, but I do want to put our mate link in place," Garrick said seriously.

Kira found her throat was dry again. What did he mean by mating ceremony and mate link?

He must have seen her confusion because he continued, "You are wondering what a mate link is. When a Catarian male first encounters his mate, both of them realise right away they are mates, and it is instinctual to want to link minds with each other. I would have preferred that you had time to know me and learn more about my people before making this decision. But we don't have the luxury of time that your friends were given. I can sense that trouble is approaching and we need to be joined to help against it."

"Link our minds? Do you mean talk together telepathically? Skylians have that ability, but we don't use it often and never with other races."

"It is similar, little mate, but has far more meaning than a simple telepathic link. It is special to Catarian people. We need the closeness of the link with our mate as it keeps us grounded." Garrick swallowed then continued, "We are a race of predators, and our mates keep us from going wild. It is hard enough when we are alone, but when a mate enters our lives nothing and no one can be allowed to harm her.

We need to touch the minds of our mates once we meet them. To not have this is unsettling."

Kira heard what he didn't say; *unsettling* was a too mild description of how he was feeling right now. She could see the beads of sweat forming on his brow as he explained the peculiarities of his race. His flushed cheeks confirmed to her that he was fighting against something.

Running a soothing hand over his arm, she found herself pulled closer against Garrick's chest. She was now draped all over him, which was fine with her. As he had been talking the rightness of this moment flooded her consciousness. Instinctively she knew this was what she'd been waiting for all her life. Maybe it was because she had never met her own intended Skylian mate that she was so accepting of Garrick's claim.

She wrapped her arms around his neck, making herself feel more secure, then leaned in and kissed him, just a little peck… for now. "You have more to tell me about the link?"

"Um, yes," whispered Garrick against her lips. "We would be aware of each other all the time once the link is in place. If you thought about me you would know where I was and what I was doing. But for it to work, you have to open yourself up to me and allow me into your mind. I will not force you to do that."

"Interesting words," Kira said absently as she smoothed the frown lines on his forehead. "You said *will not* force me, but I sense that you could if you wanted to. Can you, Garrick, can you make me accept the link without my consent?"

Drawing back to look at him, she waited for his reply, knowing that his answer would help her make her choice.

Chapter Six

Jilla shadowed the group of Skylians as they came nearer and nearer to the clearing she had chosen as her meeting place with her mate. The combined group of Jageri and Leopai stalked them, making sure they were going in the direction they wanted.

She was waiting for Garrick's signal, but the suddenness and abruptness of his mind touch startled her.

I am dropping the illusion of my mate being with her group, Seer. Good hunting.

He didn't even wait to make sure she heard him. One minute there, the next gone.

Just like the illusion.

She didn't have to pass on Garrick's comment as the shouts the Skylians made when the illusion vanished were loud enough they would probably be heard at the Leopai stronghold.

"What!"

"Where did Kira go?"

"*Skyla*, Kira."

Jilla watched as her mate touched the pad on the back of his hand.

"Kira, come in. Girl, you are in so much trouble if you don't answer me! Kira?"

She hated the distraught look on his face, but she would make it up to him… somehow.

"Soren, take the rest of the team toward the compound as we decided. I'm going to retrace our path to see if I can find Kira." Keevan ran his hands through his short hair as he talked to one of his men.

His companion laid a hand on his arm in sympathy and said, "Do you want anyone to go with you? You don't know what you'll find when…"

Keevan looked away as the other man's words trailed off. The pain on his face made Jilla's heart stop beating for a second. She saw him compose himself before turning back again.

"I'll be enough of a search party, and she'll be all right. Well, until I paddle her backside for frightening me like this!"

The others in his party gave a little chuckle at his attempt at lightness.

"Meet up with the others, and everyone carry on this path. Don't go into the compound until I return with Kira."

"It will be as you ordered, Major. Come on, everyone, we have our orders," Soren said then turned away from Keevan with the others following after, giving her mate a final worried glance.

Do you need any help to make sure your mate goes toward the pool, Seer?

Jilla was startled when one of the Leopai, Andre she thought, came up silently beside her. He towered over her in his black shifter form.

Are you not needed to keep watch over the others?

No, we are breaking up into groups. I can help you herd your mate then join the others afterwards.

Then I welcome your assistance. I was wondering how I could get him to the pool, and be there waiting for him at the same time.

Let us help you, Seer.

Another Leopai male joined them. Jilla was surprised that the two of them wanted to help her. Her surprise must have shown on her face.

Come, we can walk and talk, Seer.

Then as the three of them padded softly following her mate, the two larger cats on either side of her smaller frame, the second male said, *We know that you find it hard to trust us, Seer, but we can see the need to have this man, their leader, safely out of the way for the present. That he is your mate is a bonus for us. Darius himself asked us to help you in any way we could.*

Jilla looked one way then the other, eyes thanking them without words. This would make her task so much easier.

After silently trailing Keevan until he attempted to go in the opposite direction they wanted, the two male cats said a silent farewell and bounded off to make sure that her mate was left with no choice but to go in one direction… the one where she would be waiting for him.

She moved swiftly and carefully toward the pool that Leah had told her about. She was looking forward to having a quick dip in it to wash all the dust and sweat off her body, before she was joined by Keevan.

As she moved into the clearing, she could see why this was a favourite of Leah's. The pool wasn't large enough to swim in, but to soak and cool you off after a hard run, it was perfect. The flowers of red, pink and purple grew in abundance around the rocks and trees that surrounded this oasis of calmness.

Transforming once more into human form, Jilla removed her tunic and laid it over one of the rocks near the water. She walked into the calm depths and waited for the arrival of her mate.

* * *

Keevan was starting to think that someone was deliberately making sure that he couldn't retrace his steps to find Kira. Every time he attempted to follow the track they had earlier made through the forest, he spied a large, black cat in the way.

As long as he followed this other path, he didn't see anything or anyone. But whenever he paused or attempted to map the area he wanted to travel -- he saw another cat.

He felt as though he was being herded.

Touching the *com* on his hand for the hundredth time since discovering Kira was not with the rest of them, he said, "Kira, do you hear me?"

Keevan felt terrible that he had been fooled by whatever it was that the natives had used to make them think Kira was with them. He should have been alerted by the fact the illusion hadn't asked questions or stopped to pick a sample of the unusual plant life.

Running one hand through his damp hair, he spotted an opening in the overgrown vegetation.

No cats appeared so he forged ahead wondering what awaited him. Keevan stopped dead as his eyes focused on the lovely clearing that opened up before him. The splashing of water had him turning his head to the right... what met his eyes caused his heart to lurch in his chest.

His dream lover was watching him from the pool.

Keevan took a hesitant step then another toward her. He couldn't take in that her presence was real and not his overactive imagination.

She had piled her long, golden blonde hair precariously on the top of her head. Her gorgeous topaz eyes locked with his, making it hard to see if the rest of her was the same as he remembered.

He found himself at the edge of the rocks that surrounded the water. As much as he tried he couldn't think of a coherent question to ask her.

Thankfully she took pity on him.

"I have been waiting for you, my mate," said his vision as she stood up, water dripping off her body.

Keevan followed a bead of water as it made its way from her neck, down over her firm breast to her nipple, then disappeared to the underside. Dragging his gaze off her breasts was hard, but he managed to focus once more on her eyes.

He saw the spark of amusement there. It wasn't an unkind enjoyment but one he was sure she wanted him to share.

Finally gaining control of his vocal cords, Keevan said, "Who-who are you?"

"I know you recognise me as I recognise you, my mate. Come bathe with me while we talk."

As she spoke she moved toward him and reached out to unzip his flight suit top. Keevan covered her hand with his, feeling the spark of electricity that flowed from one to the other at this small touch. Raising his eyes to meet hers, he saw the same desire that he knew was showing in his.

Keevan thought his capacity for logical thought had deserted him on seeing his dream become reality. She was a real person -- the heat from her hand under his confirmed that. But how was this possible?

She pulled away from his touch and resumed unzipping his top, then pushed it off his shoulders and leaned into him, breathing deeply. "At last I can feel and touch you, my mate."

Keevan felt her warm breath touch his nipples, making them tighten into taut nubs. She gave each a little lick before raising her head and stretching up to kiss him.

The realistic dream earlier, now his vision become reality, was too much for Keevan. He pulled her wet, slippery body against him and covered her mouth with his. He demanded a response from her. Nothing else would do at this moment.

She moved her arms to wrap them around him, unintentionally scraping her nails over the marks his dream had left behind.

Breaking free at his hiss of pain, she said, "Turn around."

Keevan did as she asked and felt her trace the wounds on his back. She touched him gently and soothingly and then said, "I left my mark on you as you left yours on me. I don't know how it became so real this last time that we carried the marks into our real world."

He turned to her with a question in his eyes, and then noticed the little bruise on her breast. Exactly where he had bitten her in the dream. "It was real. *You* are real." Keevan knew he must sound like a flaming idiot expressing the obvious. But nothing in all his years had prepared him for this moment. "Tell me your name. We never exchanged names before."

"My name is Jilla. I am the Seer of the Jageri pack of Catari."

"Jilla. A lovely name for a beautiful woman. My name is Keevan. I'm the leader of this expedition to find our two missing women. Do you know if they're alive and well?" Before anything further happened with Jilla he needed to know the fate of his promised mate.

Jilla stepped back into the pool again. "Come and sit with me, Keevan. I'll tell you all I know of Ashley and Leah." She sat down again in the water, looking at him expectantly.

Keevan drew in a deep breath, toed off his boots, unzipped his trousers carefully so as not to catch his hard cock, and removed them. Then taking a leap of faith he stepped into the water and made his way toward Jilla. "Tell me. I need to know they're all right."

"They both had injuries from their crash. Leah's were only minor and Mata, the Leopai Seer, was able to heal her with the help of herbs." Breaking off, she moved closer to him, taking his hand in hers, then continued, "Ashley suffered a broken arm and a serious head injury."

At his startled reaction she covered his mouth with her hand to still his questions. "It's all right. She is completely healed now. Let me continue, please." At his nod she stated, "Thankfully help was at hand in the arrival of my Alpha and Shaman, Jarod and Jeran of the Jageri pack. I am their Seer. They had a vision of the crash and we made our way here, to the Leopai stronghold."

Keevan broke into her explanation, unable to keep silent any longer. "Why did they have a vision of the crash? What is Ashley to them?"

Jilla stroked his arm, as though to give him comfort. "They are the mates of Ashley, Keevan. They healed her head injury. If not for them she would still be in a coma."

He heard the truth behind her words. Why on Skyla he didn't know, but he believed everything she had told him. How did he feel that Ashley had forsaken their bond and taken not one but two native mates?

"I know this is hard to take in. Ashley has accepted Jarod and Jeran as her mates. They went through the mating ceremony yesterday."

Keevan let his head fall back against the grass covered rock at his back. Sighing he said, "As long as she is alive and well, that is the main thing. I love her like a sister, and know that is how she viewed me too. So I have no unrequited love issues, if that is why you and your people arranged this little encounter."

He felt angry at the thought that his dream lover had been used against him this way. Why hadn't they met them when they landed instead of arranging his *meeting* with Jilla?

"No, that is not why I'm here with you. Please, don't think that I would use you in that way," she said shakily. "This was my idea. I knew you were my mate, and wanted to meet you on your own without the rest of your people present."

Keevan raised his eyes to hers. He could see the truth of her impassioned speech.

Reaching out and catching her shoulders, he pulled her toward him until she had a leg on either side of his. "Thank Skyla. I thought for a minute this was going to turn out to be just a ruse."

He kissed her then, a long passion-filled kiss, her tongue hesitantly twisted around his as he put all his pent-up feelings into this show of passion. Breaking free he asked, "Is my sister unharmed? Do you know where Kira is?"

Jilla ran her finger over the deep furrows on his brow. A smile turned one side of her mouth upwards. "Kira is well. I'm sorry about the worry you have had for her, but it was necessary to separate both of you from the rest of your party."

"Why?"

"Kira's mate, Garrick, is with her. She is…"

Keevan frowned as her voice trailed off abruptly. From her expression he had the impression she was talking to someone. If that was true then the natives of this planet used telepathy. He waited impatiently for her to finish.

Jilla's eyes refocused on him. "That was Garrick; he was passing along a comment that Kira made to him. He said she was worried about the reaction of the male who had been promised to Leah. Do you feel the same?"

Keevan's stomach gave a jolt. He hadn't thought about Jason in all this. But why worry about Leah, when it was Ashley who had joined with a native… unless… "Has Leah mated with one of your people too?"

"Oh sorry, didn't I mention it? Yes, she has joined with Darius, the Alpha of the Leopai. This is his land you are on now."

Closing his eyes against the sudden pain in his head, Keevan said, "Then in that case I wouldn't like to contemplate Jason's reaction to the loss of his self-advancement."

"I have to let the others know about this threat. I won't take long." Jilla reached out her mind toward the Leopai stronghold and Jeran.

Jeran, is Leah with you?

Jilla? Yes, we are with some of the other women, waiting for word about the Skylians. What is wrong?

Garrick contacted me concerned about Jason, the male that was the promised of Leah. His mate and mine both feel that he could be dangerous once he realises she is now out of his reach.

Fuck! That's all we need. All right, I'm going to get everyone inside. I was waiting until I heard from Jarod that the group was within distance of us. But this is too important to ignore.

Take care, Jeran. I don't like the undertone of what my mate did not say about this person.

So your mate is the male who was Ashley's promised?

Jilla heard the concern for his mate in his voice. It tore her heart out to cause such pain in her friend. But she had as much right to claim her mate as he did his.

Keevan has accepted that Ashley has mated. He has said to me that he loves her as a sister. Was that not how Ashley described her feelings for him?

There was a delay in Jeran's reply.

It's not that I don't believe them, Seer, as much as I could not stand to have this man around, not one who had meant so much to my mate. I know it's selfish, but it's how both Jarod and I feel.

Although Jeran was just confirming her own thoughts and fears, Jilla felt tears flood her eyes at his words.

I understand, Shaman.

Opening her eyes, she saw the worried look on Keevan's face.

"What has upset you so much, Jilla?" he said as he ran a finger over her lashes and caught a single tear on the tip.

"I have warned Jeran about the threat to Leah. He'll make sure they are protected."

"That's good, but what did he say to upset you?"

"Nothing I hadn't realised earlier when I understood that you had been the promised mate of Ashley." Jilla swallowed before continuing, "I might not be able to remain with my pack if we mate. My Alpha and Shaman would never feel secure if we do."

At her words Keevan's cock pushed up against her belly where it was trapped between their bodies. "You keep mentioning that I am your mate, Jilla. Tell me what it means to your people." Keevan kissed her gently then waited for her reply.

"I -- I know from our dreams that you are my mate. It's like we have been together for days and not just over an hour. We of Catari only have one true mate. Not everyone is lucky enough to find the one who complements them. I had given up nearly all hope before I started to dream of you." Jilla tried to express her feelings for this man who had won her heart in their dreams.

"Sit up, darling. I need to be inside you so badly," said Keevan before clasping her around her waist and lifting her off his lap until his hard cock was at the entrance to her pussy.

Jilla reached down, took hold of his cock and fitted him inside her. She sank down, inch by inch, until she felt full to overflowing from his thickness.

When he started to thrust upwards, she stopped him by saying, "No, Keevan, you have to listen to me first. Please, this is important. You can't spend your seed in me until we go through a mating ceremony. This is really important to my people."

"So as long as I withdraw before I come, we can make love? I expect a full explanation afterwards, Jilla, but I can't stop right now," he said huskily, as he resumed thrusting into her.

Jilla kissed him, trying to say without words what his compliance and what his presence in her life meant to her. He rewarded her by breaking free and bending his head to take one hard nipple into his mouth, sucking strongly on it, and then moving toward its twin. Running her hands through his hair to keep him in position, she felt tears of joy flow from her eyes as she came.

Her internal muscles contracted as she felt his cock piston faster and faster inside her. His breathing became choppy as he too neared his completion. Jilla slowly came down from her orgasm to find him gently stroking her damp hair from her cheek. She lifted herself up and off his still hard cock and knelt down in the water in front of him.

Keevan stood up to make it easier for her to take his cock in her mouth. She took hold of him with one hand and caressed it back and forth before taking his ruddy tip into her mouth. As she sucked strongly, his thrusts became faster and he went deeper into her mouth. She opened as far as she could and tried something she had never done before; she swallowed on his next thrust and managed to take her mate's cock deeper than before. The feel of her throat and the squeezing of her hand threw Keevan into his release and Jilla swallowed his come as quickly as she could.

When his spurts finished, he pulled free from her mouth and brought her up to stand beside him. They kissed with all the pent-up feelings of love that was in their hearts, then Jilla laid her head on his chest and closed her eyes in contentment.

Chapter Seven

Garrick tightened his hold on Kira and tried to think of how to tell her about his mental powers without frightening her.

"Yes, I could very easily set our mate link in place without your consent. But I would never do that for many, many reasons," he said huskily.

This was becoming an endurance test. He was desperate to be inside her and having to focus on explaining his culture was becoming excruciatingly difficult. The pain level wasn't helped by having a steel hard cock to contend with.

She stroked his brow again. Her touch was soothing to his heated skin, but he needed her reply to his question.

"Will you allow me to set the link in place now, Kira?" He didn't know what he would do if she refused. He wouldn't blame her if she did, not with the rushed courtship he had given her.

"For some reason I would trust you with my life, Garrick. My mother had a touch of empathy which I seem to have inherited. You have a powerful mental gift, don't you? I'm not afraid. I think I am putting two and two together here."

He caught her lips with his own and gave her a brief kiss.

"What have you put together, little mate?"

She laughed. "Don't look so worried. If we are to become mates, then we need everything out in the open. Before you appeared I had a visit by this lovely big cat, who liked to purr. When he was beside me I felt a *tickle*, for want of a better word, in the back of my head." Kira paused and looked at him with an arched eyebrow before continuing, "When he disappeared, who came in his place but Garrick, who also likes to purr when stroked. Am I getting warm?"

"You are boiling," said Garrick, closing his eyes, not wanting to see disgust or mistrust in her eyes.

"Oh, Garrick, please don't shut me out. You have been in my mind since you met me, haven't you? How was I not aware of you before now?"

Looking into her pale green eyes, he saw only concern and anticipation -- not anger as he had feared.

"I have always been able to enter other people's minds without their knowledge. It's not something I do unless it's necessary to protect my pack. But it's amazing what you can find out, especially when you find your mate." Giving her a grin he said, "I especially liked your thoughts about my bottom."

Kira blushed, remembering how one-track her thoughts had been when she was walking behind him earlier.

"I think you know what my answer is, Garrick. Yes, put the link in place."

She broke off as he didn't waste any time after hearing her consent. He kissed her and at the same time entered a part of her mind that had never had any outside presence in it before. He laid down what looked like silken strands in that little corner of her mind. Strands that she followed to their end, secured in a part of Garrick's mind that she knew had never been explored by anyone.

She watched as the strands grew and multiplied, then glowed a shimmering gold. When that happened, her body began to tingle, starting with little ripples of movement in her mind that extended down her face and gradually over her body. Her heart gave a little lurch as though it was looking for something to attach itself to.

She felt Garrick! That was the only way to describe it. She was aware of what he was thinking, of his body's reaction to holding and kissing her. Never before had she felt so special, so cared for. But from linking with Garrick she knew how he saw her, how much he needed her in his life.

How utterly powerful he really was!

Breaking free from his kiss, she opened her eyes, startled to find she saw a golden aura around him that hadn't been there before.

"It's all right, Kira. It will fade shortly. It's not often that this happens, but with your empathy and my gifts, the mental side of the link manifested in the physical world."

He laid his sweat dampened head against hers. "Can we make love now?"

Kira started to laugh. She was perfectly aware of the pain he had been feeling while explaining things to her. And she was glad that was easing… now to ease his other ache.

Should she tell him that she had never done this before? Wait, he probably knew that anyway. Sneak.

"I am not a sneak."

"Huh. What are you doing now if not sneaking into my mind?" Kira felt only joy at the ease she felt with this giant of a man. She knew her initiation would hurt at first, but had no concerns that he wouldn't make up for that with the pleasure.

With a big grin on his face, Garrick laid her down on the forest floor, and knelt between her legs.

"I don't think I can wait to come inside you, Kira."

"Then don't, my love. I am wet already from your loving earlier. Please, come to me." Kira opened her arms and welcomed his weight as he placed the tip of his cock at the entrance to her pussy.

He entered her slowly, one inch at a time until he came across the barrier of her innocence. Looking down at her he said, "This will hurt a bit unless you let me take the pain from you."

"No, love, I want to feel you making me yours. Hurry, I ache for you."

He pulled out, then slid back again. It was surprisingly not as painful as she expected. Wrapping her legs over his hips, she dug her heels into his buttocks. "Please, Garrick, I need you to move now."

He immediately started an in and out motion that took her breath away. The sensation of his filling her pussy was delicious. The feel of his muscles under her hands stirred her to play a more active role, so she stroked her fingers over first one male nipple then the other. Garrick's groan at her touch emboldened her to reach up and take one little nub into her mouth and gently nibble.

His thrusts became frenzied. A wonderful warm and tingling sensation moved from her nipples and ended in her womb as her pussy muscles clamped down on his cock. Once her orgasm faded she realised that Garrick was still hard, and very still in her pussy. He looked as though he was fighting his own rush to pleasure.

She remembered his comment about not spilling his seed in her this time.

"Garrick?" she said, rubbing his arm gently.

He smiled down at her. "Ready for more?"

"I couldn't, but what about you? You must be bursting to come."

With that he pulled out of her. "Turn over onto your hands and knees."

She obeyed him without question and felt the wet tip of his cock at the entrance to her pussy once more. He pushed in and out slowly at first, then faster and faster. She saw the advantage of this position as she felt his possession so much deeper than before. In fact he touched the entrance to her cervix with his thrusts.

He pulled and tugged on her nipples, until she was shaking with her impending orgasm. She called his name huskily as she came around his throbbing cock. She was aware of him withdrawing from her pussy then the hot spurts of his come on her lower back as he too achieved his pleasure. She collapsed on the ground with Garrick wrapped around her, wondering how she could have gotten as lucky as she had.

Chapter Eight

Jilla and Keevan left the pool and dried themselves with Keevan's top before putting on their clothes. She loved the fact that he left off his shirt; she would never get tired of looking at his muscled chest and trim body.

Just as she was going to ask him if he would allow her to put the mate link in place, Jeran contacted her.

Jilla, where are you? There is trouble here. Leah has slipped out to meet up with the Skylians. There is also trouble brewing among their party. Seems that one of them is changing your mate's orders and ignoring the protests of the other. We need the two of you here… now!

Jilla clutched Keevan's arm as she listened to the Shaman.

"What's wrong, love?"

Holding up a hand, she said out loud and telepathically, "Why did Leah leave the stronghold? Did you not explain Keevan and Kira's reservations about Jason?"

Keevan wrapped his arms around her when he heard her question, running a soothing hand over her back.

Yes, but it seems he showed a far different side of his personality to Leah than he did with the others. She couldn't accept that he might cause her any harm. She wanted to be the one to tell him that she was happy with Darius and was staying here.

"We'll be there as quickly as possible, Jeran. Have you contacted Garrick yet?"

No, I was just going to do that now. I was hoping that your mate could talk some sense into his people while the two of you travel here.

"I'll ask Keevan to contact them to find out what trouble Jason is instigating. We'll be there as quickly as we can," said Jilla, breaking off at the curse Keevan spat out on hearing her comment to Jeran.

"I knew I should have left him on the base ship. He's been nothing but trouble since we got here. What else did Jeran say?"

Jilla quickly explained and learned that Keevan had a repertoire of phrases she had never heard before.

She left him to the unpleasant task of contacting his people to find out what exactly was wrong. Jilla saw the worried and angry look on Keevan's face as he returned to her side.

"Soren is fuming that Jason has ignored my orders. To make it worse, when everyone refused to follow him into the village where your people are, he threatened them with court martial and went himself. They have no idea where he is now, and more worrisome, they haven't seen Leah. I think it's time to get the other shuttle and crew down here. There is no telling what mess the bastard will create."

Jilla nodded and nibbled on her lip while he communicated with someone called Xavier.

After he finished he said, "They'll be here as soon as they can. With the extra manpower we'll quickly neutralise this threat to your people and mine."

"Keevan, we have to put our mate link in place. I feel we need that security."

"Mate link? Are we not mates now apart from the ceremony you mentioned?"

"No, this will bind us mind to mind. We would be aware of each other at all times by just a thought. I think we should do this now." Jilla shivered as she explained.

She wanted as deep a link with Keevan as she could, especially when this was getting to be so personal with Jason.

"I agree. Do it, now!"

Jilla kissed him deeply, then looking into his green eyes, she reached out with her mind. She laid her first amber-coloured strand. It flowed from one mind to the other, multiplying as it went, until the network was a maze of glowing amber. She became aware of Keevan's intimate thoughts as the last link was fixed securely in place.

He loved her.

She had known that from their dream sessions and from their loving a short time ago, but to have the actual physical proof there for her to see brought tears of joy to her eyes.

"Ssh, baby, I know -- I feel the same, but we don't have time for this now... unfortunately. We have to take the quickest route to my people. I presume you know a shortcut?" Keevan released her from his tight hold.

Taking a deep breath, Jilla wondered how to drop the next surprise on her mate.

That she was a shape shifter.

"A shape shifter? You can shift into what?" Keevan asked her in surprise.

Jilla glanced at him, relieved he didn't seem to be upset in any way by this revelation. She had forgotten how a mate can pick up your every thought unless you closed off a little part of the link to keep your personal thoughts just that -- private.

"I think it's best for me just to show you. Then we can be on our way." Dropping down onto the ground, Jilla started her change. Hands and feet became paws, and arms became legs. Bones popped as they reshaped themselves into her animal form.

Once the change was complete she stood waiting for her mate's reaction.

Keevan knelt down in front of her. "Amazing. That was the most astounding thing I have ever seen, baby. You are as gorgeous in this shape as you are in your human body." He reached out a steady hand and stroked her head, then scratched behind her ears.

Jilla smiled to herself, purring at the touch of her mate. She should have known he would be accepting of her shifter form!

We have to go, Keevan. There is no telling what will happen if we don't go to your people.

"Lead the way, Jilla," he said standing up. After collecting his pack he followed her back into the waiting forest.

They walked silently along a path that Keevan hadn't been aware of previously. He asked questions that came to him now that he knew there were shape shifters on this planet.

"I take it that the black cats that led me here are also shifters?"

Yes, they helped me out by making sure you found me.

"Are they from a different group than your own? They are a different cat species as far as I can recall."

They are Leopai, part of the Pantheri pack. This area is controlled by Darius; he is the mate of Leah.

It felt good to have this time to share information with Keevan. There was no telling what might be needed at a later date. They had walked about halfway to the stronghold when there was a rustling of the bushes behind them.

Turning swiftly, Jilla felt the reassuring mind touch of Garrick, then saw the most amazing sight -- Garrick in his shifter form with a grinning woman on his back. Kira, she presumed.

That was confirmed by the cry of joy that left Keevan's throat.

"Kira, thank Skyla!"

"Keev, oh have I got a lot to tell you."

We don't have time to stop and chat; talk as we walk.

Jilla silently agreed with Garrick's autocratic order and nudged Keevan to start walking again.

She saw the look he gave the large cat that was Garrick, and knew they would have an interesting conversation together at a later date. Not just about his command, but because of his trick earlier.

Garrick growled when Kira started to get off his back. Shaking her head, she rolled her eyes at Jilla. Jilla laughed to herself. She knew she was going to like Kira as much as she loved her brother.

"Keev, this is my mate, Garrick. Love, this is Keevan, my brother. You know, I never thought I would be introducing my husband when he was in this shape," she said with a giggle.

Kira, behave yourself. We have to be alert to any kind of trouble.

Jilla knew that Garrick only projected his reprimand to them all so that they focused on the immediate problems.

Kira just smiled, then clasped his mane and scratched behind his ears.

Jilla made a sound that would have been a laugh in human form, but came out like a cough. Keevan shook his head; he was obviously aware of his sister's effervescent personality. She had a feeling that Garrick was going to have to lighten up and not be so serious in future.

As they moved ever nearer to their objective, the mood of their little group became quieter and more serious. Kira said, "I hope Leah's all right. I don't want to contemplate what he might do once he knows all his scheming has been for nothing."

When we get to the stronghold you will stay with the other females, Kira. Then your brother and I will approach your people to see what they say.

Jilla saw the look on Kira's face at Garrick's words. She could tell right away there was a big argument looming.

Taking a deep breath and mumbling what sounded like counting under her breath, Kira then said, "Garrick, I know you are trying to protect me, but what you don't understand is that I am a doctor, a healer. If something has happened to Leah, then the technology at my disposal might be the quickest thing to heal any injury."

"I have to agree with Kira. She is a wonderful doctor, Garrick. She wouldn't be on this search party otherwise. And with both of us there we can keep watch over her to make sure she doesn't get into trouble," Keevan stated, glancing over at Kira and Garrick.

You think the situation might call for the use of your medical training?

Glancing at Keevan and seeing his nod, followed by Kira's affirmative answer, Garrick remained silent for a short time. *Very well, you'll accompany us to your people. What about you, Seer?*

Jilla waited to see if Keevan would answer in her place, but was glad he left the decision to her. *I'll come with you. I'll stay with Kira and if there is any trouble we'll both go to safety.*

"Are you shifting or staying in your animal forms? Just that it might be best to shift before we reach our people. No telling how they will react to you if you change in front of them," said Keevan.

We are close to them now. I think it might be wise to shift, Seer. They are surrounded by the combined group of Jageri and Leopai. Not that they realise that yet. Darius has picked up Leah's scent and is following it along with a few of his pack.

He stopped after his speech and Kira dismounted and walked over to Keevan. Jilla started her change. When she was finally in human form she saw that Garrick had claimed Kira's hand and pulled her toward him.

"Which way do we go?" asked Keevan, putting an arm around her.

"This way," Garrick said.

Shortly afterwards they heard the rumbling of voices, then saw some of the Jageri and Leopai sentries. Moving through the greenery Jilla saw about six people dressed in the same uniform as Keevan, talking and gesturing.

They stopped when they saw the four of them. One broke away from the others and moved to meet them.

"Thank Skyla you found Kira. And that you are here. Jason has gone too far this time. He blatantly ignored all your instructions and was a breath away from shooting Dane when he refused to accompany him. If we hadn't collectively forced him to back down..." Soren let his voice trail off, but they all realised what might and could have happened.

Keevan clasped his shoulder. "You did your best and followed orders, Soren, as did the rest of you. Well done for defusing a tense situation. Now which way did he go?"

Garrick watched his mate's companions as her brother questioned them. He was impressed with the way Keevan was both praising and controlling this situation. He would be a good man to have by his side in an emergency.

He took his attention away from the group of Skylians when he heard Darius's mind voice. He drew Kira into the conversation to keep her apprised of what was happening.

We have found where Leah met up with someone. It looks as though there was a struggle. One set of footsteps leads away from the scene. We are following the stench of this man, but would like backup of his own people, Garrick.

Pulling Kira into his embrace, Garrick replied, *Keevan is organising his group here and has called for further help. I don't think we'll need them as we are quite well equipped to handle this human. But I sense that there might be potential mates on board their ship and wanted as many as possible down here.*

Kira gave a start at his reasoning behind encouraging more of her people down to the surface. He put a finger over her mouth to stop her asking any questions at present.

Ah, I did wonder if we would be fortunate enough to procure mates for more of our people. Darius broke off, then said with a growl, *Blood, and it's Leah's. We'll need your mate, Garrick. Kell will tell you where we are. All I know is that if she is seriously injured he's dead*!

Kira broke away from Garrick at hearing of a possible injury to Leah. She took off her backpack and sorted out her supplies as he informed the group what Darius had said.

The roar of the second Skylian shuttle entering the skies above them drew their attention, and Keevan gave instruction on a closer landing spot after talking to Jarod, who had joined them. By then they all had been informed of the situation and knew where to find Darius.

They all turned with one purpose and one purpose only… find the traitor and rescue Leah. With the remaining

Leopai and Jageri still in their shifter forms, they moved as quickly and silently as they could.

In a relatively short time, they met up with Darius, who had tracked his mate and her kidnapper to one of the little pools of tranquillity deep in the forest. They watched as Jason shook an unconscious Leah. When that didn't wake her he filled his water bottle with some of the water from the pool and flung it in her face.

The low growl that came from Darius caused the party of Skylians to shiver and take a second look at his face. His eyes were shining silver with rage.

Then Darius held out his hand to catch their attention.

Leah is awake but pretending she's still unconscious. She says the blood was from the cut on her head. The traitor hit her when she refused to go with him. She is sorry she didn't believe what she was told.

Garrick made sure that the group of Skylians heard. From the looks on their faces they weren't used to having their minds taken over like this. *Can she move or has she been injured in any other way?*

He waited for Darius to answer. From his expression he was hearing better news, as his eyes were returning to their normal shade.

She is well, apart from the cut on her head, and wants to know what we want her to do.

Garrick conferred with Darius and Jarod. They included Keevan in their four-way conversation. When they had decided on the best way to tackle the rescue, Keevan broke away and with a soft voice explained to his people.

Jason had no time to even aim his gun, as Jageri and Leopai shifters converged from all sides and surrounded him. He couldn't even use Leah as a shield because with a command from Darius she rolled away and shifted into her cat form.

The look on Jason's face as she turned snarling at him was quite comical. He peed his pants at seeing the gentle woman he knew turn into an animal that could tear him apart with ease.

Leah turned when Darius reached her side, changing back into human form. He pulled her into his arms and squeezed her until she protested. Then he let her go and let Kira examine her head, which she fixed quickly with a little gadget from her pack.

When he was sure that Leah was completely well, Darius picked her up in his arms, saying, "Never again will you disobey either me or another when we are looking after your well-being."

Leah cupped his face in her hands and said, "I'm sorry I didn't listen to Jeran and Ashley. This is the first time that I've ever seen Jason in this light. He's always been the perfect gentleman with me, never raising his voice. I couldn't comprehend how dangerous he is. I thought if I explained it to him, everything would be fine." She shivered. "I can't believe he was the same person I knew on our ship. I am truly sorry, Darius. I will apologize to Jeran and Ashley when we get home."

She turned her face into his neck then. Darius kissed the top of her head. "An apology would be good, but it's not going to get you out of your punishment. I must have lost about five years of my life when I saw your blood."

Garrick turned as Kira walked up to him. "I think you might have left a little thing out of your explanation, mate!"

Knowing full well she was referring to Leah's ability to shift, he wrapped his arm around her shoulders. "I would have explained well before our mating ceremony, Kira.

Things have happened so quickly since we met it's a wonder that's the only thing I missed."

Keevan turned when he heard the ending of his explanation. "I take it that I'll be a Jageri as you are, Jilla?"

At her nod, he shook his head and said, "No one will believe this on the base ship. The fact that we are embracing this change will make them feel antipathy toward us." He turned back to his crewmates. "Once we meet up with Xavier and the others we'll discuss what's to be done with our prisoner. Of course you realise neither Kira nor myself will be making the return trip with you." At their nods he said, "Then let's follow our hosts back to their home. I think we all need a good stiff drink."

Chapter Nine

Kira got a warm welcome from Ashley when she entered Leah's home. Her handsome mate was the mirror image of his brother, apart from not having a scar. Ashley looked as though she was extremely happy with the way things had worked out for her. At least she was after she saw that Leah was well.

Kira was glad Ashley took Leah off to one corner and gave her a lecture. They might have distracted her from hearing what was said by these fascinating shifters. When they met up with Xavier and the others, Soren had drawn them to one side and explained what was going on. The funny looks she was getting were to be expected, she supposed.

Maybe she should have a word with Keevan about sending the more sectarian members back to the ship with Jason. It would be a good idea to get him off planet and locked away. Although she wouldn't blame him, she didn't want Darius to take matters in his own hands about meting out punishment. That was for Leah's father to do, as it was his daughter the crime was against.

Seeing that Keevan was talking quietly to Xavier, she went over to join them.

"Keev, it might be a good idea to send some of the -- less tolerant crew back to the ship with Jason. Then you can take your time to record your report for the commander."

Xavier smiled at her. "Just what we were discussing, Kira. As much as I hate to say it, I think Darien and the others should go before they hear too much about your plans. Once Jason is off planet I think these people will have some interesting tales to tell us."

Thera came to join them. "Let me stay, Major. I find this fascinating. Did Leah really transform into a cat?"

Kira smiled at her friend. "Yes, nosey, she did. I am glad you're all right with all this. I am surprised at how well the majority of our people are accepting it."

Xavier sighed. "I think you are finding that a good many of us are fed up with the restrictions that we live under, Kira. I know you are, and so were Leah and Ashley. That's obviously why they accepted their situation here so readily. It leads to interesting questions about whether more of us should strike out on our own."

He was interrupted when Garrick, Darius and Jarod came over to join them.

"We need to talk about exactly that. Send the uneasy ones of your people away. Then we'll talk," Garrick said then motioned for her to join him.

"Come, we need to freshen up."

The wonderful bathing room that Mata, the Leopai Seer, took her to and the tunic that she was given made her feel so relaxed and at home with these people.

Mata took Kira to the dining room. She found there that the Skylian contingent was reduced to ten, including herself and Keevan. That the ones who stayed were on Keevan's regular crew list was not a surprise. He was such a charismatic leader his crew was willing to follow where he led -- even in such strange circumstances as this.

Garrick smiled as he saw her standing by the door, and beckoned her over to sit with him. The fact that Jarod and Darius were also there told her that important things were being discussed.

When she reached Garrick he pulled her down on his knee. She was quite happy to be close to him. Even that short time apart had been too long.

Darius looked around the table. "Good, everyone is here. First I want to say thank you for your help in recovering my mate. And for your acceptance of our nature. I know from what Leah said this is not easy for you, so thank you for being prepared to listen with an open mind and heart."

"Now it's my time to tackle something that is not so pleasant to me, but my brother and I feel we need to say it." Jarod turned to Jilla and Keevan. "We are happy that you have found your mate, Jilla."

"I sense a *but*, Jarod," Keevan said.

"We are sorry, and yes, ashamed of ourselves, but we could never welcome you into our pack, Keevan. Not with the relationship you have had in the past with our mate." Holding out his hand to Jilla, he said, "I am sorry, Seer, to have to say this, but your home is no longer with the Jageri pack."

Jilla's eyes shone with unshed tears. Keevan drew her onto his lap, glaring at a red and shamefaced Jarod.

"No, Keevan, it's all right. I expected this when I realised who you were. I don't hold Jarod or Jeran to blame for feeling this way. I don't want you to either."

"Maybe once we are secure in our relationship with Ashley we could welcome you both. But we can't find it in us just now." Looking up at them both Jarod said, "I truly am sorry. We'll do everything in our power to make sure you are safe and secure somewhere else. Darius and Leah have tendered an invitation to stay with them until you decide what to do."

"I have a solution to this problem," Garrick broke in, "if you are willing to hear me out. I can't authorise this unless I have the agreement of Darius and you, Jarod."

Kira leaned forward and took Jilla's hand in hers, and gave it a squeeze. Garrick had left his thoughts open to her, and she thought it was a fantastic idea. She hoped the other Alphas agreed.

"We all know some of the systems at the City are failing. We don't have the knowledge now to repair them. But from talking to Keevan, I think he can. And maybe if some of our other guests here wish to stay, they would be equally as helpful to us." Garrick broke off and waited to see if there were any questions so far, before continuing. "Another thing that has been of concern to me is that when our duty shift is over, we leave before the next pack arrives. There is no continuity; we leave recordings of what has still to be looked at, but what I propose is that we have a caretaker pair there all the time, or to be precise, Jilla and Keevan."

Everyone started talking at once. Kira kissed Garrick on the nose for his brilliant idea. It would mean that she would see Keevan frequently.

Jarod said, "You would be happy with this arrangement, Jilla? You will be mixing with every pack at different times."

"I would be more than happy with this, Jarod. But -- would this be acceptable for you and Jeran?"

"It would be more than acceptable. Our time is not for many moons. By then we'll feel more secure in our feelings for Ashley. It'll be good to have you among us again when the time is right."

Kira smiled at the happiness flooding Jilla's face.

"I agree to this arrangement too," said Darius.

"Thrice agreed. Where is your Shaman, Darius? We need to seal this pact."

Jeran walked in the room with Aaron, the Leopai Shaman. "We'll both seal this pact. I think this is a wonderful idea, Garrick. Thank you."

She was fascinated by the complex ceremonies these people had. She watched as the three Alphas' palms were cut, then they all mingled their blood. Both Shamans joined hands with the three of them, and witnessed the agreement that would allow Keevan and Jilla to be permanent residents at this mysterious City. Then when Jeran and Aaron took away their hands, the three cuts had healed themselves, apart from a red mark.

Amazing.

She wasn't the only one fascinated by these so vastly different people. Thera could hardly contain her excitement, and once everyone had retaken their seats she said, "I want to stay; in fact I feel I *have* to go to this City with you. Do I have your permission to remain on your world?"

Keevan said, "It's fine with me. Thera is a good pilot as well as a good technician; she would be a help with maintaining your damaged systems."

His words opened a flood of questions and requests from the remaining seven Skylians. All who were at this meeting wanted to remain. It didn't matter if they found out that there were no mates suitable for them from the Catarian peoples. They just wanted the freedom of this wonderful planet.

Keevan groaned. "I better get started on my report, then we can upload it to the ship in orbit. The controls of the remaining shuttle can be put on auto-pilot, unless anyone who didn't make the trip down here decides they want to stay with us."

"Don't send it up yet," Garrick said. "I intend to wait until I'm with my people before joining with Kira. Why don't you all use it to transport yourselves to the City, then send it up?"

"That makes perfect sense to me." Keevan glanced at Jilla with a nod. "Jilla and I would like to have your people witness our joining too, if that is all right?"

Kira grinned and said, "That is more than all right, big brother. We wouldn't have it any other way. When can we go to meet our people, Garrick?"

Hugging her, Garrick said, "I think we have had enough excitement for tonight. Tomorrow we'll all travel to meet my pack."

The evening drew to a satisfactory close, and they all retired to their bedrooms. Kira took off her tunic and pulled down the sheet covering the bed. Garrick came and stood behind her, and lifted her hair away from her neck, giving her little nibbles and kisses, until she turned around to face him for a kiss.

She would never get enough of this man's touch. Just a simple kiss and already her pussy was wet and ready for him.

Breaking free, she kissed his throat, then down to his nipples. Giving each some attention, she followed the trail of sparse hair down to his belly button, which she blew on, then continued her way down, loosing his loincloth to expose his engorged cock.

The tip had a small bead of white sitting on it. Kira licked it up, loving the salty taste. She continued to lick around the bulbous head, then taking his hard length in one hand, pumped it in time to her sucks on the tip. Garrick's groan made her eager for more, but he broke away and swung her up and laid her down on the bed.

She didn't want to wait until he joined with her, and she wasn't slow to tell him so.

"I want you inside me now, Garrick."

He looked up from sucking one nipple. After running a finger over her labial lips and discovering she was sopping wet, he moved over her and positioned his cock head at the entrance to her pussy.

"I love you, Kira. You are everything that I ever dreamed of in a mate." Then he plunged into her waiting depths. The thick cock filled her and without any further stimulation, she felt her orgasm start. Her nipples hardened further. A shiver went down through her body and culminated in her womb. The contractions of her pussy took her breath away, and she stiffened for one moment as the overwhelming pleasure reached its peak.

The hot splash on her stomach told her that Garrick hadn't needed much more time to reach his satisfaction either. As he collapsed on her, she wiped his damp hair from his brow and gave him a kiss. Garrick caught her hand in his and kissed then licked her palm. She had just had a satisfying orgasm -- how could he make her burn for him so soon?

Kissing his way down her neck, he took one red nipple in his mouth, suckling gently. Letting it pop out, he moved down to where he had left his own signs of his orgasm. Kira couldn't believe it when he started to lick her clean. The purring sounds he made when he headed down to her pussy sent shivers throughout her whole body. She shook with need by the time she felt his hot breath on her clit.

Garrick fastened his mouth on that little bundle of nerves and pulled and rolled it with his tongue. Kira reached down and ran her fingers through his hair as she moaned his name.

He purred and blew on her clit. Inserting two fingers in her pussy, he finger-fucked her while nibbling on her clit. Faster and faster, in and out until she groaned out his name as she saw stars.

When she was calm once more Garrick crawled up to join her on the bed, and took her in his arms. Kira turned toward him and fell asleep in her mate's arms, content for the first time in her life.

Chapter Ten

Jilla woke up to the feeling of a tongue on her pussy. Closing her eyes once more at the delicious sensations running down her lower body, she opened her legs further for Keevan.

Thanks. You taste so good, Jilla.

Jilla smiled at the ease with which Keevan had taken to their intimate mind link. He was discovering it came in useful at times like these.

He inserted one then two fingers and pushed them in and out as he licked and then nibbled on her clit. Then a third was added and he fucked her with them. Taking his mouth off her clit, he moved up until he could suck on her nipples at the same time, keeping his fingers moving in and out of her pussy.

Jilla ran her hands over his shoulders, loving the feel of the body hair that covered Keevan. She could feel her orgasm start, from the stimulation he was providing. Her body shook as her pussy walls contracted around his moving digits.

He removed them once her spasms had stopped and lifted himself up and over her. The stretching feeling as his thick cock entered her pussy caused another flood of cream that eased his way inside her.

Keevan bent down and kissed her. She tasted herself on his lips, their flavours mixed into an aphrodisiac that had her digging her nails into his shoulders.

Please, Keevan, move. I need you so much.

I love you, Jilla, but can you take your nails out of my back?

Jilla pulled away from his kiss and looked into his eyes, seeing the humour shining back, and stroked his mangled shoulder soothingly. "Sorry, you just make me wild."

Keevan began to move, in and out, then changed his position to get a different angle. It gave her so much pleasure. She lifted her legs and wrapped them around his waist. He was able to move deeper into her than before, and increased his pace as his breathing became choppy.

With a shout she felt him withdraw, and the warm flush of his release splashed over her pussy and belly. Her own orgasm contracted and squeezed her womb in time with his spurts of come.

Keevan collapsed at her side, slinging an arm around her and pulling her tight against him. Still breathless he said, "Are you sure you are going to be all right? I want you to be happy."

She smiled. "It's the best thing that could happen, Keevan. Garrick was right when he said that a lot of the systems need repair. We don't know how to keep them running. That's one of the drawbacks to the arrangement we have. There is no communication of vital information, so it's been lost to us all."

"Don't worry. With the crew I have we'll soon get things going again. I have to say I'm looking forward to the challenge," Keevan said, then leaned over and kissed her. It started out as a gentle kiss, but soon changed into one of passion.

Jilla pushed him down on the bed until he was lying on his back, then moved up and over him until she was straddling his thighs.

She bent down and licked his small nipple, drawing it in her mouth and sucking strongly. His musky male scent filled her senses as once again she felt her passion growing for this man. Jilla knew that no matter how much they made love, it would always be like the very first time.

Kissing her way down his body, she arrived at his semi-hard cock. Taking it in her hands, she stroked gently until it hardened beneath her touch. Jilla slithered down until she could take the tip into her mouth. Savouring his taste, she ran her tongue over the underside of his cock, and then sucked for a few minutes. She ran her tongue and teeth lightly over the tip then down the side of his cock and back. A little bead of pre-come leaked out and she sucked it up, purring with pleasure at the taste.

Releasing him Jilla once again straddled his hips, but this time she took his hard cock into her waiting pussy. Steadying herself with her hands on his chest, she moved up and down with increasing speed.

Keevan groaned, "I didn't think there was any way I could go again so soon, but your taste and scent does something to me, Jilla. But maybe this isn't the best position for me to withdraw, love."

Jilla recognised the logic behind his comment. She would be so happy once the mating ceremony was over and she could feel the hot splash of his seed where it belonged... deep in her pussy. She reluctantly moved off Keevan and knelt on the bed beside him.

"Take me from behind, Keevan. If I can't feel you coming in me, then at least I can take you deep this way."

Keevan gripped her hips, then slowly pushed his cock into her. The feeling of fullness at this angle was amazing. He made short strokes, and then longer ones as his breathing grew harsher. Jilla's body shook as the pleasure became overwhelming. He was touching her cervix with his thrusts and the pleasure/pain along with the friction of his cock threw her into a satisfying orgasm.

His masculine groans as he withdrew from her pussy, then the hot splash on her buttocks as he reached his own satisfaction, thrilled her.

They collapsed on the bed, and Keevan drew her back into his arms, kissed her lightly then sat up, pulling her with him. "Come on. I'm eager to see my new home, and to say goodbye to my past."

After refreshing themselves they met the others for breakfast. Plans were confirmed and before she knew it, they were standing in front of the Skylian shuttle saying goodbye.

She found it hard not to cry when she hugged Jarod and Jeran.

Ashley did cry. "I wish things could be different."

But Jilla felt a weight had lifted from her shoulders. "I have trained two girls who will be able to take on the duties of Seer for the Jageri. It isn't as though they can't contact me if they're unsure of something."

"But you're leaving your home."

"As long as I have Keevan by my side, I am home."

* * *

Damon of the Unicorni backed deeper into the trees as the two shuttles closed their doors and lifted off the ground. He was pleased with the way the cats had evolved and grown. The way they handled the challenges that were put in their way made him smile.

Touching the small protrusion on his forehead, he contacted his companions in the Leopai stronghold.

They are reaching the stage that we hoped for, learning to work with the different packs in order to reach a satisfactory conclusion. Do you agree?

Yes, brother. We can see the day coming when we can show ourselves to them in our true form without fear that they'll attack without listening first.

Then it is agreed. We wait to see how they cope with the Skylians' help. If this venture they have initiated works, we'll reveal ourselves to them.

In the stronghold, two of the horse-like creatures the Leopai used for transporting their belongings nodded their heads in agreement.

Kyla Logan

Writing erotic romance with the full support and encouragement of her family, Kyla Logan lives on the east coast of Scotland. Along with her sons and her own life mate of many years, she lives in an area full of historical interest, in particular, the fascinating remains of standing stones left by the Picts, who lived in the area so many centuries ago. An avid reader from an early age, Kyla loves reading paranormal erotic romance, from shape shifter to vampire, mermaids to futuristic. Other hobbies include spinning, making paper, and some stitching techniques. The ideas that have been running through her head for years are finally making their way onto the computer screen, thanks to the encouragement of two dear friends, and of course, her husband. Visit Kyla at http://www.kylalogan.com

Changeling Press E-Books
Quality Erotic Adventures Designed For Today's Media

More Sci-Fi, Fantasy, Paranormal, and BDSM adventures available in E-Book format for immediate download at www.ChangelingPress.com -- Werewolves, Vampires, Dragons, Shapeshifters and more -- Erotic Tales from the edge of your imagination.

What are E-Books?

E-Books, or Electronic Books, are books designed to be read in digital format -- on your computer or PDA device.

What do I need to read an E-Book?

If you've got a computer and Internet access, you've got it already!

Your web browser, such as Internet Explorer or Netscape, will read any HTML E-Book. You can also read E-Books in Adobe Acrobat format and Microsoft Reader, either on your computer or on most PDAs. Visit our Web site to learn about other options.

What reviewers are saying about Changeling Press E-Books

Aubrey Ross -- Club Carousel: A Taste of Twilight

"Full of scrumptious bliss, A Taste of Twilight charms you into reading its pages before delivering spine tingling satisfaction... If you love vampires who rule the roost and passion that burns brightly then this book is a must buy because not only does it have those qualities but also it makes for a fantastic read."

-- Sheryl, Ecataromance

Mardi Ballou -- Third Time's the Charm

"This story is loaded with sexual tension that isn't relieved until so close to the end that you'll be screaming in frustration."

-- Scarlet, Realms of Love

Ruth D. Kerce -- Undercovers 3: Illicit Behavior

"Filled with suspense, humor, and erotic passion. I was engrossed from the first page and stayed glued to my seat until it had ended. Ruth D. Kerce did a tremendous job!"

-- Jessica, Fallen Angel Reviews

Lacey Savage -- In His Dreams

"I was in suspense as to where the ending might go and was very happy to get what I wanted (nope, not going to give it away!). Definitely a must for all paranormal fans."

-- Glenda K. Bauerle, The Romance Studio

Willa Okati -- Dante's World: Black Leather Night and Other Tales

"I just love Willa Okati's work. She writes funny and darkly erotic tales about vamps and other paranormals; she is entertaining without ever losing the black edginess that characterizes her work. She is also not afraid to lavishly detail and find the beauty in homoerotic intimacy. Black Leather Night and Other Tales is a treasure; a trio of tales skillfully crafted and served up for your pleasure. Enjoy!"

-- Michelle, Fallen Angel Reviews

Marteeka Karland -- Forbidden

"Ms. Karland does a wonderful job of drawing you into the story. She keeps your attention throughout with the plotline, the paranormal element and the big surprise she throws in along the way. I must say I for one am looking forward to what use she will put her imagination to in the future and would thus, like to recommend Ms. Karland's Forbidden to those of you who like erotic science fiction romance."

-- RogueStorm, Fallen Angel Reviews

Shelby Morgen -- Northlanders 1: Way of The Wolf

"One powerful read. The reader can practically feel the magic in the air, along with the impending dangers. The long list of characters spins a yarn that keeps the reader on the edge of their seat. Ms. Morgen has composed a well-written fantasy that vividly depicts a story that stays within the heart long after it is finished."

-- Jessica, Fallen Angel Reviews